# CASSIE MINT

# Grumpy Suits: An Office Romance Collection

BLACK CHERRY

PUBLISHING

# Contents

I  Silver Fox

Description                                              3
Kara                                                    4
Galen                                                  11
Kara                                                   18
Galen                                                  24
Kara                                                   31
Galen                                                  41
Kara                                                   48
Galen                                                  54

II  Sweet Tooth

Description                                            63
Julian                                                65
Lola                                                  74
Julian                                                83
Lola                                                  90
Julian                                                96
Lola                                                 105
Julian                                               113
Lola                                                 122

Julian                             133
Lola                               141

III   Filthy Headlines

Description                        149
Sasha                              151
Grant                              157
Sasha                              164
Grant                              173
Sasha                              183
Grant                              191
Sasha                              200
Grant                              208
Sasha                              219
Grant                              227
Sasha                              234
Grant                              247

*Teaser: His Last Nerve*           251
*About the Author*                 257

# I

## Silver Fox

# Description

**H**e's older and wiser. A king in a three-piece suit. And there's a secret side to him that only I see.

High above the city in this office in the clouds, I serve the best man I've ever known. Galen Onasis is a legend—a titan of industry. When he gives an order, hundreds of workers snap to attention. They scurry away from him in the halls.

But when we're alone, there's another side to my boss. He doesn't bark orders at me—he speaks softly. Sweetly. I *live* for his quiet praise.

Would the legend ever want a girl half his age? Gosh, I hope so.

Because I can't go on feeling this way.

# Kara

⚜

The only warning I ever get is the whir of the elevator. It's sleek and almost silent, perfectly built like everything else in this building, so I keep my ears trained for the slightest whisper; for that ten-second warning when the golden elevator light begins to glow, racing through the floors.

I don't play music. Don't put in earbuds or hum as I work.

I like to know when he's coming.

Not because I'm scared of Galen Onasis—which is kind of funny, because everyone else definitely is. When he prowls the lower offices, glancing over shoulders at computer screens and pulling managers aside, the air is so thick with trepidation, you'd think our boss is a bonafide tyrant.

He's not, by the way. At least, not to me.

Though ever since I became Galen Onasis' executive assistant three years ago, Human Resources has insisted on monthly meetings with me, just in case. They sent me a special holiday card last year, with a handwritten note to *Reach out anytime!'*, as though Galen has me trapped up here like a princess in her tower.

When I pass the HR team in the halls, they stare at me like they're waiting for a secret signal—for me to blink twice or tap S.O.S in morse code on my thigh.

They'll be waiting a long time, because I'm no damsel in distress. I *love* being up here with Galen. Sometimes, when the sun shines through the huge skylights and low-lying clouds hug the skyscrapers, it feels like we're in our own private world.

This morning when the elevator hums, I glance across the office, my reflection staring back at me in the shiny silver doors: a wide-eyed girl with a pressed peter pan collar, my thin bracelets clinking as I arrange my boss's breakfast on his desk.

Black coffee with a small jug of milk on the side. One pink grapefruit, halved, with a sharpened spoon. A glass of room temperature water, and three vitamin supplements laid out ready.

Guess this explains how Galen looks like *that*, even as silver threads through his brown hair and bleaches his temples. The man's a Greek statue. A pin-up model. He's just so *disciplined* about everything, his toned muscles testament to how hard he works in all areas of his life, and setting out this severe breakfast every morning makes my chest pinch.

When will Galen Onasis allow himself small pleasures? When will he finally relax the iron grip on his self control?

I bite my bottom lip, placing my personal addition to the breakfast: a bran muffin on a small, white plate, fresh from my oven at home. Galen didn't ask for this, but I'm offering it. Trying to tempt him.

No, it's not healthy, but it's still bran. The softest possible fall from grace.

As the elevator doors *whoosh* open, I scurry back across to my own desk. This is an open plan office, with the whole sun-drenched top floor reserved just for Galen and I. Well, us and the dozens of olive trees Galen keeps in huge planters. They grow beside the huge windows and under the skylights, leaves curling in pleasure in the golden sunshine.

Every morning when I come up here, it's like the elevator doors part and I step into a dream. A mythical kingdom, or a fairy tale lair.

But when Galen steps off the elevator, he huffs loudly and marches across the tiled floor, tugging at his shirt cuff.

"Morning, Kara."

Even in Galen's stormiest moods, he still greets me warmly, and every time it makes my head spin.

I grip the edge of my desk and offer him a smile. A *normal* smile, with an appropriate amount of excitement to see my boss. You know: none of the tragic yearning I feel for him on display.

This is why I like advance notice that Galen is coming. Why I listen for the elevator. I need to batten down the hatches; get my stupid crush under control.

"How did the meeting go last night?"

Galen grunts.

Oookay then. Not great. "Well remember, *you're* the one with everything they want. You hold all the power, Mr Onasis."

A faint smile drifts over my boss's handsome face as he passes my desk, crossing to his own and sinking into the leather chair. He's in a tailored gray three-piece suit, his waistcoat hugging his trim waist. Galen's old school. "You're right. What would

I do without your pep talks, Kara?"

Ha! Um. How about: become a titan of industry. Try: build an award-winning film studio and amass a huge amount of wealth. Galen Onasis was a legend long before he ever met me.

Meanwhile, I'm a twenty-six year old assistant getting paid to lay out this man's breakfast, and I burned a whole batch of bran muffins before I made the final version on his desk. He didn't say it in a mean way, but I sink down behind my desk all the same.

*Me*, giving Galen Onasis pep talks. Can you believe it? So ridiculous.

"What's this?"

My boss nudges the bran muffin an inch away with the tip of his finger, his mouth flattening in distaste. Sudden regret is a stone lodged in my belly.

"Uh." I clear my throat, and my cheeks are on fire. "I thought maybe you'd like something different this morning. A treat."

Galen wrinkles his nose at the muffin I baked him, his doubt clear. Yep, I want to die.

"Forget it." My desk chair clatters as I shove to my feet, hurrying across the tiles to his side. I snatch the muffin so fast, crumbs spray over the desk. "Shoot. I'll get those in a second. I'm just—hang on."

A strong hand wraps around my wrist, holding me in place, his skin bare against the sleeve of my cardigan. Such a big hand, with strong, squared knuckles and a sleek watch clasped beneath his cuff. As my boss watches me closely, the pad of his thumb dips beneath my sleeve, resting against my brown skin and tracing circles over my pulse point.

My traitorous heart pitter-patters so fast. I'm a rabbit caught in a snare.

"Sir?" I squeak.

"Where did you get the muffin?" Galen's frowning at me, suspicion etched on his brow. This is his lie-detector thing. He might as well hook me up to a polygraph.

And god, I should extricate myself, but he's so handsome when you get this close—his face is made up of such clean lines, it's like he could be etched from stone.

Blue eyes narrow. "Kara?"

It's no use. Galen sniffs out lies better than any bloodhound. "I..."

What can I tell him? *I baked it for you. You work so hard, Mr Onasis, so I wanted you to have some sweetness in your life. And I ate so many muffins myself that I made myself sick, all because I wanted to taste what* you *would taste.*

Even sitting down, Galen's face is level with mine. His hand is so warm and steady on my wrist.

"I baked it," I whisper, radioactive with embarrassment and shame. Because who does stuff like this? What kind of executive assistant brings her all-powerful boss squishy baked goods from home? Maybe HR *should* have me on some kind of watch list.

"Thank you."

Just like that, Galen releases my wrist, and I suck in a shaky breath. What is he thanking me for, exactly? My humiliating confession, or my ill-considered gift? I move to step away, but he plucks the muffin from my hands—and it's even more misshapen now. Lumpy and tragic.

"You really don't need to—"

Galen takes an enormous bite, holding my gaze. He's eaten half of the muffin in one go, his strong jaw shifting as he chews, and I'm so mixed up right now. So embarrassed, so nervous, so thrilled. "Is it… okay?"

Galen swallows and nods, then eats the rest of the muffin in one bite. And I guess that's my answer, though it doesn't tell me what I really want to know.

Like: should I bring him muffins for breakfast every day now? Did he actually enjoy it, or was that a pity bite? Did he feel my pulse going crazy when he held my wrist?

Is my boss as desperate for these stolen touches as I am?

*No.*

Meetings. Agendas. Notes.

There are a thousand things I should be thinking about right now, and none of them are baked goods or the rugged line of Galen Onasis' jaw. I'm not paid to moon around after my boss, damn it, I'm paid to make his life easier.

"You have a meeting at ten thirty, Mr Onasis, and Casting sent up more suggestions for your final approval. Also, *Titan* magazine called again, and they really want to do a profile on you. They promised the front cover and a six page spread."

Galen rolls his eyes, and I press my lips together, fighting a smile. He hates doing magazine spots, even though they raise the profile of the studio. Says he feels like an idiot getting dressed up and told to pose.

Galen Onasis doesn't admit things like that to anyone else. He saves those pieces of himself for me.

"You think I should do it," he says flatly, and I shrug. My cardigan sleeve brushes against his shirt, but I still don't step back, not even as warm tingles race over my skin below the fabric.

He touched me first. He started it.

And I'm testing my luck here with this unspoken game,

nudging a toe across a line, but Galen doesn't send me away. If anything, his desk chair creaks as he wheels a fraction closer.

"It's a major magazine," I point out. "And you wanted to find new ways to market the streaming division."

"Alright, alright." Galen dumps milk into his coffee, expression sour. "I'll do it, Kara."

My laugh is nearly silent. A choked puff of air. We're still so close together—so near that if someone walked in right now, they wouldn't know *what* to think. "You don't have to do what I say, you know. I'm not the boss, Mr Onasis."

Blue eyes flick to me, then away. "Sure you are."

And I have no idea what that means, but I float all the way back to my desk, warmth swirling through my limbs. Galen ate my muffin, and he agreed to the magazine feature. He called me the boss.

See, everyone on the lower levels may be frightened of this man; they may whisper about him in the break rooms and scuttle away when they see him coming.

But *I* know what he's really like behind closed doors.

And the big, scary boss? He's a pussy cat.

# Galen

❧

"Quarterly figures look good, and we've brought on a lot of new talent. By this time next year, we could be looking at..."

I frown down the length of the meeting table, letting the updates about my company fade into a steady drone.

I *know* all this. Do they think I'm completely ignorant about my own business? There's no analysis to these words; no fresh angle I might not have considered. It's basic, and these overpaid managers are like eager school children, bringing scribbled reports to their teacher and hoping for a gold star.

I need to shake up my workforce. Trim the excess, then recruit.

A stolen glance at Kara chases the irritation away. She's hiding a smile, taking diligent notes in that looping handwriting of hers, and I *know* she can sense me wrestling with my temper.

I've offered her endless gadgets for her note-taking. Laptops and tablets and dictaphones and god knows what else. Hell,

I've even offered to hire Kara her own assistant, but she insists that handwriting everything helps keep her attention sharp.

She was downright outraged at the assistant offer, too. That was a relief. I don't want another person working on our floor with us.

I like our time alone.

And maybe *I* should take handwritten notes in these meetings. Perhaps then I could focus on something other than my assistant for more than five minutes at a time.

"We think you'll be very pleased with our new casting process, Mr Onasis—"

"Do you?" It's harsh to interrupt him this way, and the manager fumbles in his speech, his grip tightening on his water glass. In my peripheral vision, Kara ducks her chin.

She's never been afraid of me like the others. I know my reputation—know they think of me as the devil in fine tailoring. That they run from me in the halls.

Even if I hadn't heard their whispers, I'm sure I could smell their fear in the air, as though I'm truly a monster and not simply a man who demands quality. Everybody wants Onasis Studios on their resume, but so few want to pay the damn cost.

But Kara… she's never frightened. Never shies away from my gaze. When I risk another glance at her now, she's watching me, a knowing glint of humor in her dark eyes.

She stood so close to me yesterday. I felt the heat emanating from her body.

Okay, I need to ration out these glances. If I loosen the grip on my control, I'll do nothing *but* stare at Kara, the rest of the world be damned. Storms could rage outside those windows and meteors could burn through the skies, and I'd still be sitting here, chin propped on one fist as I catalog every detail of my assistant.

She's in a pale pink cardigan today, buttoned over a white blouse. A gray pencil skirt is hidden beneath the desk, and the pale colors of her blouse and cardigan are striking against her smooth, brown skin.

Kara brought me a lemon poppy seed muffin this morning. So buttery and sweet, with a tang of citrus. Delicious.

Her cheeks darkened when she saw me lick the crumbs off my fingertips.

"Give me your projections," I tell the room, but I'm still looking at Kara. I play these idiotic games with myself when meetings get dull: setting limits on the amount of times I can look at her, but then privately decreeing it only counts as one glance so long as I don't look away.

I bet *she* knows what's coming down the pike for this company. Kara may be an assistant, but she's also the sharpest mind at this table.

I include myself in that analysis. Perhaps once upon a time, I'd have been quick enough to give her a run for her money, but that was before she joined me in the penthouse office. Before everything in my brain reoriented toward *her*, my thoughts tilting toward her like sunflowers tracking warmth and light.

Fuck.

It's a good thing these assholes can't hear my thoughts. No one would be scared of me anymore, that's for sure. I've gone soft since meeting Kara.

And this isn't the best room to hold my focus, anyway. In between the huge windows and the panoramic view over the city, large mirrors dot the walls. Everywhere I look, there she is, taking notes and smiling at a private joke. Making my heart skip and my stomach tighten.

"Let's wrap this up."

I want to steal Kara away back to our private floor. Want her all to myself, where she might stand next to my desk again and tease me with that soft voice. Where I can watch her stride through the olive trees to the copy machine and back, her hips swaying with each step.

So maybe my assistant *should* be afraid of me, just a little. Because god knows I'd never hurt her, but this hunger I feel near her, this buzzing, heightened awareness, this obsessive need to watch her and cater to her every comfort...

That can't be normal. Certainly, I've never felt this way before.

"Of course, Mr Onasis," someone says.

*Kara Onasis.* The name floats across my brain, unbidden, and I pinch the bridge of my nose. Why would I think that? Why would I even let myself go there? Fucking hell.

She's a beautiful, clever, sweet young woman, and suitors must surely fling themselves at her feet everywhere she goes. Meanwhile, I'm a notorious asshole and nearly twice her age. Never mind that I'm also her boss. Thinking of her like that... even letting myself *think* it...

Pathetic. I might as well doodle her name on my notepad.

"Sir?"

My chair scrapes against the floor and I stand quickly, smoothing down my waistcoat and tie. "Forget it. Send me the rest by email. Reach out to Kara if you have questions."

Several men stiffen in their chairs, affronted by the idea, while the female managers purse their lips but nod. Less fragile egos.

And I don't care about wounded pride—Kara can handle any issues these people raise. She knows the company inside out, and she can predict my decisions with eerie accuracy.

"Kara?" Her name comes out clipped, my tone strained, but only because I choked back a dozen other names for her first. *Sweetheart, princess, darling.* They all come so naturally to the tip of my tongue when I'm looking at her. HR would have a field day. "Let's go."

Despite my frazzled mood, Kara rises gracefully, tucking her pen into her notebook's spiral binding. Her black hair is smoothed back into her usual bun, but two shiny locks have been left free, curling against her cheeks.

I want to twirl them around my fingers. Want to feel their softness against my knuckles, and gently tug.

Want to guide her pretty mouth down my body.

"You know my extension," Kara tells the room, and then we're gone, striding through the corridor toward the elevator. I'm too impatient, making her hurry to keep up, so I shorten my steps to keep her from running in her heels.

But I'm eager for our shared office; our olive trees and skylights. The vanilla scent of the candle she keeps on her desk.

I want to get my assistant alone.

It's a drumbeat in my chest. A sharp need, slicing through me, eviscerating my restraint. Fuck. I hold out until we round the first corner, both safely out of view, then I grip Kara's wrist and tug her closer; I seal our bodies together and press my assistant against the wall.

And I can't explain what I'm doing. My brain is silent, running on pure instinct.

When I touch her, I feel such relief.

I've done this so many times to Kara in my dreams, touched her so many different ways in my brain, that I guess my body thinks it's normal. Because I'm touching her, gripping her, cruising on autopilot. Feeling the sweet perfection of those curves against my hard lines.

"Galen," Kara gasps, blinking up at me, her eyes wide. She tugs on my arms, pulling me closer.

But god, I'm crushing her—pressing up against her like a goddamn caveman. My trance shatters as quickly as it came.

I stumble back, horrified. Where did that come from? What is wrong with me?

It's not bad enough that I practically bite my fist every time Kara walks into a room—now I'm pawing at her in the halls?

No. No, Kara deserves better than this.

I'm too old for her. Too bitter.

I've got no fucking right.

"Actually, I have a meeting." My voice sounds tinny, but at least the words make sense. I stride the last few feet to the elevator doors, my assistant following slowly behind me. I jab the button for her and then step away.

I need space. Need to clear my head, and to get myself together away from Kara before I do something we'll both regret.

Can't believe I touched her like that. Can't believe I felt her fucking heartbeat through my clothes.

My *assistant*. I'm such an ass.

"Across the city," I lie. "It's not in the calendar."

Delicate eyebrows pinch together. Kara's still thrown off by what just happened, but her gears are turning and she's catching up. "Oh. That's weird. Why…?"

"Because it's personal," I snap, then my insides plummet as Kara jerks back, startled that I've lashed out. Who can blame her? First I crush myself against her, then I bark.

Hurt fills her pretty brown eyes, and this is no better than her blushes and confusion a few seconds ago. Not at all.

"I won't be long," I say, but she's not looking at me anymore. Kara has turned away, pressing the elevator button again like that'll make it come sooner. Her mouth is pinched, and she's smoothing down her freshly-crumpled clothes.

I did that to her.

God.

"Thank you for the muffin this morning," I say as the elevator rumbles closer. It's so inane, but I'm desperate. I can't walk away with this new tension crackling in the air—I need to get us back onto familiar ground. *Safe* ground, where I'm a good boss and I keep my damn distance. Where I don't make her blush, and I *definitely* don't hurt her feelings.

"You're welcome," Kara murmurs, and then the elevator dings. The doors swoop open, the gilded box empty, and I should step in there with her, but I don't.

It's a long ride to the top floor.

And I've just proven I can't trust myself.

# Kara

The next morning, Galen is cool and collected when he steps off the elevator, resplendent once again in a white shirt and blue silk waistcoat. There's no hint of the weirdness between us yesterday; no nod to the split second that he held me, nor harsh way he'd said, *"It's personal,"* right after. No acknowledgment of the fact that he didn't come back to the office at all after his mystery meeting.

It had to be a date, right? What other 'personal' meetings can stretch for the whole day with no explanation?

My stomach lurches. I set my coffee mug down with a dull thump.

His body felt so right against mine. I can never unfeel that.

"Any messages?" Galen asks, his tone as brisk as his movements. He breezes past me, barely sparing a glance in my direction, the faint, spicy scent of his cologne lingering in his wake. And it hits me in one sickening go: my boss is trying very hard to show his complete lack of interest in me. He's dismissing any idiotic hopes that might have bloomed after yesterday.

It was a mistake. Obviously.

Why did I get so freaking fluttery over it all?

Imagine if Galen knew that I touched myself while thinking about him last night, trying to remember every detail of his scent, his heat, his form. Imagine the look of horror and disappointment that would surely settle on his handsome face.

Ugh.

I'm such an idiot about this man.

"Casting called again for your final decision, and *Titan* magazine is scheduled for next week." I sound like a robot, but at least I'm professional. No meltdowns here, no way. "There's also an issue with one of the prop warehouses. I put it all in an email."

"Thank you, Kara."

Kind words, but in a clipped tone. Galen's chair creaks as he sinks behind his desk, and he still won't look at me for more than a split second at a time. Instead, he narrows every ounce of his attention on the cuffs of his sleeves, rolling each methodically back to the elbows and smoothing them into place.

Tanned forearms appear slowly, corded with strength and dusted with brown hair. Why is that sight so stirring against his fancy waistcoat?

My mouth is dry as I glance around this huge, empty office; the secret grove of olive trees with no other humans in sight. Nowhere to hide and no distractions, either.

Finally, Galen turns his focus to his breakfast. He pauses at the lack of muffin, but says nothing about it.

Okay.

Everyone hates their job sometimes, right? And I've had

three years of interest and excitement; three years of challenge and fun. Three years of swapping secret smiles with Galen Onasis, and wandering this skyscraper with a private thrill that the big, scary boss *likes* me. That he trusts me more than anyone else on his staff.

I'm overdue a rough patch. And my bruised feelings are not my boss's problem, just like his maybe-date is no business of mine.

But: "Where were you yesterday?" I hear myself ask.

As soon as the words escape my mouth, I grip my pen in both hands, squeezing so hard the plastic creaks. I sound like a jealous girlfriend, not his assistant. So humiliating.

*It's personal.* I wait for the rebuke again.

Instead, Galen spins a grapefruit half and picks up his spoon. He's frowning, his broad forehead pinched, as he stares at his super healthy breakfast. "I needed a moment."

After what happened in the hall? Does that mean he didn't have a date? I *need* to know.

"Alone?" I rasp.

Blue eyes bore into mine. I shiver, the pen creaking in my grip. "Yes," my boss says at last. "Alone."

I should feel better, but I don't. Because all of yesterday afternoon, I missed Galen so badly, and it's a good thing this office is tiled, because I would've worn a hole in the world's sturdiest rug with all of my pacing.

And I'm still mad at him for the way he spoke to me, and embarrassed about that fact, and I've lost all track of what's normal and what's not.

We've always had a strange relationship—closer than the usual boss-assistant bond. We've been confidantes. Friends and allies. And I've always loved that fact, but now I wish there was a manual for this conversation.

Galen pushes to his feet with a sigh. He nudges the plate with the grapefruit halves away from the edge of his desk, spinning the spoon around until it's at three o'clock. He always does that.

"I don't even like grapefruit," he tells me as he strolls across the office, hands tucked in his pockets. "Too sour."

He's getting closer. Those broad shoulders brush against olive tree branches as he walks, the leaves whispering against his fancy clothes. Are they soft? They look like they might be.

"Why do you eat them, then?" My palms are clammy around this pen. Does this confession mean we're okay? It feels like we're reading the lines for one conversation, but really having another.

A broad shoulder shrugs. "I'm an old man, Kara."

"Not *that* old."

"And if I don't take care of myself, I'll age even faster." His tone is light, but Galen's eyes are solemn as they watch me. He comes to a stop right in front of my desk.

Silence. It's heavy in the room, weighing down on my shoulders. My chair creaks as I shift.

I don't know my line; don't understand this script. Galen needs to help me out here.

And sure enough, "I hurt your feelings," my boss says at last. I shake my head, but he doesn't believe me. I can tell. Neither of us is any good at lying to the other. "Forgive me, Kara. I shouldn't have snapped like that, nor lied about having a personal meeting. I should have told you I needed to clear my head."

Well… yeah. I guess.

But did he really need to clear it alone? Away from me? I

know I sound nuts, but Galen *always* talks through his troubles up here. I have the boss's ear; the king's confidence. I'm a smug little jester like that.

And I desperately want to ask what was bothering him, whether it was our almost-embrace in the corridor, but he didn't confide in me yesterday, did he? And he offers no answers now.

Instead Galen stares at me, those pale eyes tracking over my French braid; the sheen of gloss on my lips; my tailored blue blouse, the same color as his waistcoat. Hey, our outfits match.

My body heats under his inspection, my nerves prickling to life. Remembering how he felt pressed against me.

My boss clears his throat and looks away.

"I'll be spending more time outside the office over the next few weeks." The words are addressed out the window, at the skyscrapers jutting into the pink morning sky. My stomach sinks. "You won't see much of me, but I don't want you to worry, Kara." Too late. "It's not a comment on your job performance."

I… what?

What is happening?

Galen Onasis won't be in the office for *weeks*, and he's leaving his trusted assistant behind, and I'm not supposed to worry? Not supposed to read between the lines?

"We'll keep in touch," he says, like emails and phone calls could replace *this*. Being in the same room as Galen. Seeing the way his clothes shift as he moves, pressing against the toned planes of his body, then falling away; hearing the rasp of stubble when he scrubs his five o'clock shadows on late nights. Watching his eyes fall closed when he takes a sip of the coffee

*I* make him.

Okay, so I shouldn't have been nosy. Shouldn't have practically swooned from a single touch. Does he really need to leave?

"I could come with you." My pen clacks against the desk as I place it carefully on the wood. My fingers are trembling, so I tuck them away in my sleeves. "Everything I do here, I could do remotely."

"No." Galen's eyes crinkle as he smiles.

Oh, my heart. Ow, ow, ow.

"But thank you, Kara."

Then he walks away, like he didn't just grind my heart into the tiles. Like he didn't give me a split-second glimpse at what it would be like if Galen Onasis touched me, then tossed me from that high into the pits of despair.

I squeeze the edge of my desk, watching my boss stroll back across the office, and I will not cry.

I will not cry.

I will not cry.

"This is for the best," Galen says softly ten minutes later, his voice floating across the room. Like we never stopped talking.

"Uh-huh." I slip my earbuds in, one by one. No point straining to hear that elevator anymore. "For the best."

# Galen

It has been six days since I saw Kara, and I deserve some kind of award. Is there an Oscar equivalent for moody employers? I'd win the self control category—apart from that one damnable slip, anyway.

Because being away from my sweet assistant for this long… it's torture. No other way to describe it.

I go to bed thinking of Kara, then wake up from dreams about her. I eat my stupid grapefruit every morning and want to talk to her so badly, it tastes twice as sour as usual.

I linger over every single email I write her like I'm crafting a sonnet, and whenever my phone buzzes, I jump out of my skin.

*Kara.*

It's ridiculous that I've been driven this low. Forced to this extreme—banished from my own office because I don't trust myself to keep my hands off her.

I bet she's found someone else she prefers already. Someone her own age.

Fuck. Don't want to think about that.

"This way, please, Mr Onasis. We're so thrilled to work with you today."

I trail a tiny woman with a black pixie cut across the *Titan* magazine lobby, draining the last dregs of my take-out coffee. Rain lashes the street outside, and my coat is wet and heavy against my shoulders.

Kara was right. This profile *is* a good idea, and not only to raise the profile of Onasis Studios. It's also a much-needed distraction; a way to keep me from pining after her all day from my apartment like a lovesick schoolboy.

They can dress me up in whatever ridiculous outfits they want, as long as it takes my mind off Kara.

"Your assistant is here already."

I grunt in response, following the pixie-haired woman through bustling corridors and past busy open plan offices. I ordered a temp from the studios to come over and make the notes that Kara usually would. They won't be anywhere near as competent, but they'll do, whoever they are.

"Eighteenth floor," my guide tells me when we reach an elevator, pressing the button as we cram inside. This building is jammed full of crowds and writhing with frenetic energy—the complete opposite to the oasis of calm in my olive tree grove. Everyone is dressed in high fashion and tapping furiously on a tablet or smart watch. "Here we go."

This is not my first rodeo. I've done plenty of magazine features before, because Kara's right: they're excellent PR. So I'm not taken aback when my guide leads me into the studio; I'm not intimidated by the giant spotlights and camera rigs and racks of designer clothing. There are dozens of people in the room, ready to watch me play dress up in someone else's clothes and glower for the camera, but that's not what stops my heart.

It's Kara.

She's dressed in a burgundy pinafore dress and black silk t-shirt, her hair smoothed into a low side bun. A laptop rests on her knee, a takeout coffee cup on the fold-out table next to her chair, and though she doesn't glance over from her spot by the wall, I *know* she knows I'm here.

Those shoulders tense. Her plump lips purse.

Kara taps away at her laptop, frowning.

"Our editors have picked out several outfits for you to choose from, Mr Onasis. If you'll follow me—"

"One minute, please."

Every step toward Kara, my brain screams at me to turn around, but I can't help it. I'm drawn to her, pulled on invisible strings.

Was it really only a week ago when I felt her pressed against my body? When her vanilla scent filled my lungs and made my head spin?

"Mr Onasis." My beautiful assistant glances up, then back to her lap. The split second her eyes are on me is a gut punch. And I was hoping for her usual warmth, her frank appraisal, the twinkle in her eye that says the two of us share a big secret.

Instead, she's cold and distant. A consummate professional, but nothing more.

"Kara," I rasp.

"The temp you requested got stuck in traffic. I'm here to fill in." Though she directs her words at her laptop screen, her voice is brittle with hurt and anger. "Hopefully we can manage."

Ah, shit.

I didn't think about how this would look—how badly it would hurt Kara to find out that I requested someone else, *anyone* else but her. She must think I blame her somehow for the line *I* crossed. That I'm holding her responsible, though the fault was all mine.

And there's no excuse for an oversight like that. No excuse for any of the bad decisions I've made lately.

I'm losing my touch. They shouldn't do a magazine profile on me: they should write an exposé.

"Kara," I say again.

"I brought a packet of your more urgent mail. The rest I've summarized in an email. Others have been asking when you'll be back in the office, but I've explained to them that I don't know."

She shoots me a glare. I deserve that. This whole situation must have been embarrassing for Kara, but nothing prepares me for her next words: "I won't be available on Monday. I have interviews all day."

The floor drops out from under me. She's leaving Onasis Studios?

Fucking hell. I want to slam my head into a wall.

"Don't go," I say, then wince at myself. At the mixed signals I'm sending. Why am I so desperate to keep her with me when I won't even allow myself in the same room? When I'm calling in temps instead of letting her do her job?

Kara clearly has the same question. Her mouth presses into a hard line. "The *Titan* team are waiting for you, Mr Onasis."

"Kara—"

"I need to make a call. Excuse me." She stands quickly, placing her laptop on the rickety table, and she doesn't even take her phone as she strides from the room.

Just like that, I'm dismissed. She doesn't want to see me. This is a disaster.

\* \* \*

"Raise your chin, Mr Onasis."

"Look here, Mr Onasis."

"Annie! Straighten his collar."

For the next four hours, I'm poked and prodded. Dressed and combed. Six different women bring me jackets and shirts, trading them out for pieces which are still warm from my body, smiling up at me from beneath their lashes.

I don't care about them. Don't care about *any* of this.

Kara won't look at me.

"Will this take much longer?" I ask between gritted teeth, a spotlight shining in my eyes and shutters clicking all around. "I have another appointment."

Kara glances up at that, her lips parting as she looks over at me, and for a second it's all there, the emotions marching across her face in a damning slideshow: surprise, curiosity, hurt, bitterness. A desperate wish for this to be over already.

And beneath all that, there it is: the heat that's *always* been there, simmering in her deep brown eyes. Energy crackles in the air between us. A silent *what-if.* I dismissed it before, wrote these stolen glances off as the wishful thinking of a lonely man, but standing on this platform and staring at my assistant, I can't deny it anymore.

It's not shallow.

Not a passing infatuation.

It's *obsession.* If Kara doesn't meet my eyes in the next few minutes, I will howl.

"Just two more outfits," a magazine worker says sweetly.

No.

Kara's shoulders have slumped, and that means I'm done here, *Titan* feature be damned. They can bill me for wasted time if they must, but I won't spend another minute watching my assistant's composure slip away.

Kara is grace personified. She's always calm and serene—a goddess. For these cracks to show, she must be more hurt than I ever realized.

"We're finished. Thank you." Eight different magazine workers open their mouths to argue, but I stride past them, hopping off the raised platform. This starched shirt is strangling me, and I tug at the collar as I approach Kara, working the top buttons undone.

"You're coming back to the office with me."

She blinks, staring wide-eyed at the bared sliver of my chest like a deer in headlights. The muscles on my back tighten as I feel her hot gaze on my skin; my pulse pounds with her so near again. Then the moment is over as, shaking herself, Kara says, "Surely *you're* coming back with *me*."

Touché.

Fine. Whatever. I don't want to nitpick, I just want this woman by my side again. Speaking to me in her soft voice; smoothing down the skirt of her pinafore dress. I want the rigid set of her shoulders to ease, and I want to inhale enough of her vanilla scent to last me another six days.

"I'll call the car around."

Kara's mouth is tight as she snaps her laptop closed. "Alright. I'll need two minutes, Mr Onasis."

So will I. To hunt down my own clothes and down a bottle of spring water; to find the nearest mirror and glare my own worst instincts into submission.

I won't push Kara away anymore, and I won't tug her closer either.

I can do this. I can be the man—the boss—she deserves.

# Kara

The car is claustrophobic as hell. It's so dark with the tinted windows; so small with its black leather seats. The air con is freezing, my skin goose-pimpling under my clothes, and the tinny sounds of the radio are faint through the driver's partition.

I've been in this car hundreds of times, but I've never wanted to scream before. Funny how quickly things change.

Galen sits beside the window, his tall, muscled frame folded into the space like origami. He's watching me, *always* freaking watching, those pale eyes shocking as they rove down my limbs.

Is there more silver in his hair already? How is that possible after only one week? Unless this week has sucked horribly for him too...

*No.* I shut that thought down before it can gain traction.

Because if Galen wanted to see me over the last six days, he could have reached out at any time. He's my boss: I'm literally at his beck and call. The ball has been in his court, and apparently he forgot I exist.

He even requested a temp today. A *temp*. My hand shakes as I rub my chest.

"Heartburn?" Galen asks, and my hand drops into my lap.

"Something like that."

His expression darkens.

Yeah, well, Galen can scowl at me all he likes, his handsome features as thunderous as the rain pounding on the roof of the car. It won't make me confide my personal feelings, and it won't stop me from going to those interviews on Monday.

I owe Galen Onasis precisely this and no more: a high quality of work between the hours of eight and six. No weekends; no late nights. I'm *done* putting my whole heart and soul into this man.

He doesn't want them anyway. My heart. My soul.

He wants a freaking temp.

"You look ready to push me into traffic."

This is my cue to laugh, to say something professional to smooth things over, but I can't do it. I just can't. So I give a jerky shrug, then stare out of the tinted glass.

I would never push Galen out of the car. Would never hurt him. But he's right—there's something satisfying about the fantasy right now. And lord knows I have a thousand and one fantasies about the man sitting opposite me, but this is the only one when he's fully clothed.

"Kara."

I've always loved and hated the way he says my name. Slowly, with so much care, like he's savoring it, his voice low and rough. A bedroom voice.

Damn it.

My mind whirls through all the things I could say, the

updates I could give him, but I blew through them earlier. I should have held some back, because now there's nothing in this car except taut silence.

"Don't go to those interviews," Galen says.

I shake my head, jaw tight, eyes fixed on the rain-slicked street. I'm going to those freaking interviews, and I'm going to nail every last one. Galen Onasis may have lost faith in my work, but I'm the best at what I do. The *best*.

I don't need him, damn it. I could have moved on from my assistant position a long time ago.

I *don't* need him. Except…

"May I put you as a reference, Mr Onasis?"

Galen's sigh is dredged from the soles of his feet. And I'm ready to argue my case, but he mutters, "Of course."

Good. I mean, I knew he would never sabotage me—Galen's not nearly as much of an asshole as everyone thinks, the last week aside. But it's still a relief to hear it. The ice around my heart thaws the tiniest bit.

"Thank you," I tell him.

My boss grunts.

*Such* a caveman. And he's looking at me like one too, his muscles tensed and jaw clenched like he might toss me over his shoulder and leap out of the car, weaving through traffic as he runs into the sunset. Like he's *hurt* that I'm leaving; like he really wants to fix whatever has shattered between us.

Never should have baked those damn muffins. No one likes bran.

The car drifts through the slow traffic, rain drumming on the metal roof, and the two of us sit in silence for the rest of the journey.

\* \* \*

"I need to explain."

Galen begins speaking the second the elevator doors hush open, marching toward his desk. I follow more slowly, squeezing the leather strap of my handbag, the weight of my laptop digging into my shoulder.

My clothes are damp, spotted with rain from the dash inside. It's coming down so hard out there, there's a thick mist clinging to the office windows. High above, the skylights rattle with the force of the onslaught.

From here, I can see the light blinking on my desk phone—I have messages waiting. Work to do.

Galen all but growls when my feet turn to my own desk. I walk there calmly, sighing with relief as my heavy bag *thunks* down on the surface.

Just like that, my boss is here at my elbow, kneading my aching shoulder with one hand, the touch so unexpected and so damnably thrilling. It's only my shoulder, for god's sake. It shouldn't make me tremble, and yet...

"I'm sorry. I should have carried that for you."

The image of Galen Onasis, powerful businessman and ruler of this skyscraper, carrying my handbag across the lobby does something weird to my brain.

"What did you want to explain?" Better to get this over with. I let myself get carried away with daydreams before, but it won't happen again. Heart aching, I slip out from under Galen's hand and sink into my desk chair. "I need to meet with accounts in an hour."

This time, his growl is loud and clear. "I own this building, Kara. I could fire the whole accounts department if I wanted to."

When Galen spots my eye roll, I brace for another terse comment. But he sighs and scrubs a hand down his face. "Fuck, this mess is bringing out the worst in me. No, obviously I wouldn't do that; *obviously* you can go to those interviews. Alright? I'm not a damn ogre. Please, Kara, have mercy on me."

And those last words are so desperate, I can't resist looking up.

Ice blue eyes bore into me, and I'm falling into their depths. I'm falling, twisting, *soaring*, trapped in the zero-gravity of my boss's gaze.

He takes a step closer. "I've handled everything poorly."

Huh. Those words aren't easy for a man like Galen Onasis to say. He's built an empire after all, crafted a huge company from the ground up. Every word he speaks comes with the ultimate authority.

I wet my lips. "Okay."

"I should never have stayed away from you like that. Should never have put that fucking distance between us." Galen's pacing back and forth in front of my desk, raking a hand through his brown and silver hair. And now that I've seen him in an endless array of strange clothes, I can confirm: the silk waistcoat and shirtsleeves combo really works for him. It *really* works.

Not that it matters.

"So why did you stay away?"

I mean, I know why: because I made things weird. Baked those stupid muffins for my boss and asked personal questions like a fool. Practically melted against him like a groupie at the first touch. But I want to hear him say it, so I'm inoculated against ever doing something so dumb again.

"I didn't trust myself," Galen rasps. "I didn't trust myself with you."

Silence rings through our olive tree grove, the leaves cast in shadow by the mist outside.

Um. What? But Galen's standing still now, gazing down at me with so much emotion churning in his eyes, and he's not done.

"If I spent one more hour alone in this office with you, Kara, I wasn't sure what I would do."

Oooh my gosh. My chair creaks as I cross and uncross my legs. I clear my throat, heart pounding. Is he really saying these things?

I must be reading this all wrong. Must be projecting or something, except when I turn his words over in my head, I can't figure out any other meaning.

He wants me. Galen Onasis—the man I've yearned after for so long—*wants* me. Maybe even as badly as I want him.

Enough to crush me against his chest in that corridor. Enough to stay away for six days straight to keep from touching me again.

And we haven't solved everything between us yet, not by a long shot, but I can't help saying, "Well. We're alone in this office right now."

Galen goes still. *Eerily* still, like a big cat eyeing its prey. His chest doesn't even rise and fall with his breath, and his gaze is fixed on me.

I've never felt this exposed before. So flayed open. Gosh, I'm warm.

I wait, but Galen says nothing. He doesn't come an inch closer; won't act without an invitation. But you know what?

I'm feeling reckless. Dizzy.

"What exactly were you afraid you might do, Mr Onasis?" I clear my throat, and try to sound assertive. "Show me."

*Now* his chest moves. My boss sucks in a deep, shuddering breath, and then he's moving, striding around the edge of my desk.

My chair skitters across the tiles as he yanks me around; I let out a squeak as he takes my waist, lifting me onto the edge of the table. A pen clatters to the floor. My phone falls off the hook.

It's chaos. Unbridled chaos.

Galen kicks my chair away like it's his worst enemy, and then he's *here*, crowding into the space between my knees.

Dimly, I remember I'm wearing a dress today. It's hitched to my mid-thighs, the fabric taut between my spread legs so he can probably see my panties, and *god*, I've never done something like this. Never let a man touch me this way.

There was always something more important going on. College assignments; To Do lists; work duties. Responsible things for responsible people. Hello, my name is Kara, and I am the ultimate goody-two-shoes.

I force a breath into my lungs. Galen's waistcoat creases in my tight grip.

"This," my boss says, squeezing my hips, my waist, my upper arms. Testing the feel of me, and it puts our rushed embrace in the corridor to shame. "This is what I was afraid I might do, Kara."

This? As in, stoke my body heat higher until I'm panting for breath? Make me rock and press against him, wanting his hands everywhere? Wishing his touch would be rougher?

Well, I can't pretend that it's a sensible idea, but the oddest thing is happening to me right now.

I just—I don't *care.* I don't care if this is not smart, because I'm swaying in Galen's grip, and my cheeks are hot, and there's an ache building below my navel. God, I've wanted this for so long. I've dreamed about it so many times.

And I don't want to be sensible. Don't want to remind Galen about HR.

I want to turn my big, scary boss into a shuddering wreck. I want to take him apart and rearrange the pieces. I want to make him need me as badly as I need him—so he'll *never* walk away from me for days ever again.

"I'm not—I don't know what I'm doing." Despite my warning, I lean forward and scrape my teeth over Galen's throat. His five o'clock shadow has come in, rasping like sandpaper, and his pulse thuds against my top lip. My boss groans.

He gathers me closer, and I'm not hard and muscled like him; not worldly or commanding. What I *am* is desperate to feel his mouth on mine.

The famous Galen Onasis does not disappoint. He tips my head back and cradles my cheeks—then pauses to run the lock of black hair I left out of my bun between his finger and thumb, humming at how silky it is.

Gosh.

His chest is solid beneath my palms. This man is a wall of heat, wrapped in fine tailoring and a silk waistcoat.

"Are you sure?" he murmurs.

"Uh." My laugh is strangled. *"Yes."*

When our lips meet, my brain goes blissfully blank. Everything fades away: the meetings I have scheduled; the many reasons that this is a bad idea; the full laundry hamper waiting for me in my apartment and the groceries I forgot to pick up yesterday. I'm so used to wandering around with my brain overheated, my mind full of open tabs, and finally, *finally*, Galen has forced a shutdown.

"Mmph."

He kisses me harder. I kiss him back.

The desk creaks as I wrap my legs around his trim waist.

"Kara," Galen groans, and his breathing is as ragged as a cross-country runner's. *"Fuck.* Princess."

Ha. Um, princess? No one has ever called me something like that before, not even when I was a little girl. I was never the glitzy, special girl; never the center of attention. I was the plain Jane with a battered library card and a shy scowl.

Heat slides down my spine like dripping treacle, and Galen's hands follow, arching my body against him. Our tongues slide together. I'm *tasting* him. Tasting my boss.

"Princess," he rumbles again.

His breath is minty. Did he slip a peppermint on the drive? You know, I don't mind his nickname for me.

"This is complicated." Galen presses the words into my neck, searing a trail across my overheated flesh. Strong hands roam up and down my back, and it's like he can't stop touching me. Mapping his territory. "I know that. Whatever you want from me, that's how this will go. Okay, Kara?"

I nod.

Whatever I want?

I want Galen Onasis on his knees in front of this desk, burying his face between my legs. I want to pull on his salt and pepper hair, and I want to feel the vibrations when he calls me *princess* right to my pussy.

But I've never—I don't know how to ask for that. And what

if it's too much? Too demanding? What if it pushes him away?

It takes forever, but I find my voice. Swallowing hard, I tell Galen, "Let's take this slow."

Sensible. Responsible. The Kara way.

You know, it may be boring, but it's never steered me wrong before. And the stakes are too high right now. I *need* this to work between us.

This man is my soulmate. It sounds crazy, but I know he is.

"Slow," Galen repeats, then he inhales sharply and nods. "Then that's what we'll do."

It's awkward, disentangling ourselves. Unwrapping limbs; smoothing hair. Galen's waistcoat is creased beyond salvation, and I laugh weakly as I try to smooth it, silently cursing my cowardly declaration.

Is it too late to change my mind? What would he do if I gripped the back of his neck and tugged our mouths together again? Would he groan against my lips like he did before? Would he suck on my tongue?

But my boss smirks at me before he turns and walks back to his desk, and for the rest of the afternoon, I chew on my bottom lip.

Soon. I'll be brave soon.

Eventually.

# Galen

Two unwelcome things land on my desk at the same time: a single typed sheet from Kara giving her written resignation, and an early proof copy of the *Titan* feature. The page layouts are unfinished with blank boxes where ads will go, and some of the taglines on the front cover are clearly placeholders.

I flip the cover page over with a groan, wincing at the title they gave me. *The Silver Fox of the Studios.* Silver fox? Me? A hand rakes through my hair, unbidden, and my throat is dry. Am I really that old?

A stolen glance at my much younger assistant makes my chest lurch. What if Kara sees this? What if the reality of our age gap finally hits her?

Her resignation letter sits near the corner of my desk, folded in crisp halves. A ticking time bomb. If I lose her now, I'll *really* lose her.

"Oh, I forgot." Across the room, Kara pushes to her feet and smooths her palms over her cranberry silk sheath dress.

She rummages in her handbag, popping a container open, and then she's coming for me, honing in like a beautiful missile, weaving between the sun-drenched olive trees.

I'm not ready.

I'm fucking—I'm *gray*.

The cover image slams face down on the desk, my hand rigid on top of it. My stiff face resists me at first, but I force it into something resembling a smile, waiting for my girl to reach me.

Kara doesn't notice. She's too busy placing a muffin in front of my keyboard.

"Ta da!" God, her grin is beautiful. Makes me want to fall to my knees and weep. "It's banana and walnut. I tried a new recipe, so, you know, set those expectations low."

She could present me with a burned husk with the sugar swapped out for salt, and I'd still eat it. Still rate it five stars. "Thank you, Kara."

Her dress rides up a few inches as she rests her hip on my desk, sifting through the morning mail that I've spread across the surface, those smooth brown legs a constant torment. Her eyes linger on her resignation note, then flick to me and away.

My smile is waxy. I may be stuck like this.

"Which job did you go for?"

"Strategy at Holmes and Co. I figure I've done enough assisting by now."

She sure has. Kara could run this whole building with her hands tied behind her back, and I'm glad that she's progressing. Glad that her talents will be recognized.

I *am*, damn it; I just need to remind myself of that fact over and over, whenever I remember that she'll be gone.

No more looking up from my desk and seeing her tapping

away at her keyboard. No more stealing kisses in the elevator like the last few days, hardly believing my luck. No more hearing her husky voice as she talks on the phone. No more *muffins*.

I'm fucking bereft, and my smile is crumbling off my face.

"You could head up Strategy here."

Kara laughs but shakes her head, still scanning my mail. I wasn't joking.

"What's that? Oh, the *Titan* piece." She spins one of the pages to face her, brown eyes zig-zagging back and forth as she reads. A sly smile curls her plump mouth. "I seriously think they had a thing for you, Galen. This profile is downright breathless. Although—hm, I'll send them a correction on that. They make it sound like you're some incorrigible bachelor."

I was, before I met Kara. Too busy with work to date, and happy that way. Now I'm a heartbeat away from ordering bridal magazines to her apartment, laying my hints on thick. Now that would well and truly drive her away.

"Tell them I'm taken." I'm rewarded with a shy smile, and my stomach swoops. Fuck, the things this girl does to me. I'm going to miss her so much.

*Silver Fox.* My hand twitches on top of the cover page, the paper crinkling and drawing Kara's eye.

"Oh, is that the front page? Here, let me see—"

"No." I drag the paper away, a side tearing. God, I am acting insane, but I can't seem to stop myself. "Don't look at that."

The look Kara gives me could shrivel my balls at twenty paces.

"Galen. They're going to sell this magazine in every corner shop and paper stand. I'm going to see it eventually, and if you don't show it to me now, I can't fix any problems."

Curse her logic. Curse her perfect brain.

Curse my own fucking arrogance at thinking I could ever keep such a gorgeous young woman. I can't even keep her on my staff, let alone in my life.

But Kara doesn't wait for me to get my head out of my ass: she pinches the corner of the cover page and pulls it from beneath my rigid palm.

"Oh." The paper is creased as she holds it up, tilting it this way and that. A frown puckers her forehead, and it deepens as she scans all the wording. "I... don't see it. What is the problem, exactly?"

*Silver Fox.*

I clear my throat, but the words won't come.

"The Silver Fox of the Studios," Kara murmurs, and it's so much worse hearing it in her soft voice. "The rest of these are placeholders, and the photo is great—"

She cuts off, pressing her lips together.

Brown eyes flick to me. To my fucking *hair.*

"Don't," I rasp. "I'm an old man. You don't have to say it."

And for the record, I have never once cared about my age before. Never bothered with a midlife crisis. I figured sneaking up on fifty meant experience and wisdom; a strategic edge that younger competitors don't have. I figured it made me level-headed when others lose their tempers. It lent me authority.

But that was before Kara. Before I fell in love with a girl nearly half my age.

What I wouldn't fucking give to be twenty years younger for her.

Kara blinks at me, and I realize I said that last part out loud. Shame and embarrassment crawl up my neck, but she pushes off the desk, tossing the cover page back into the mess of my mail.

"You think you're old, Galen Onasis? That's nonsense." Heels drum against the tiles as she rounds my desk, then the shoes skid away across the floor, both kicked off with very un-Kara-like abandon. "Silver Fox doesn't mean gray. It means sexy. Distinguished."

Is this the most mortifying pep talk she's ever given me? Possibly. But Kara pushes my chair around to face the side, then sinks to her knees.

"The floor will be cold—"

"I don't care."

Fuck. What happened to taking it slow? Where is the gorgeous but prim woman I've been courting, never progressing beyond a few heated kisses?

Not that I've minded. A kiss from Kara is worth a lifetime with someone else. But still, as two palms stroke along my tensed thighs, my brain is muddled, my thoughts as slow as if they're wading to me through thick mud.

"HR," I begin, and Kara snorts, reaching for my belt buckle. I watch her fiddle with it, blinking down at my lap in a daze.

Then finally, *finally*, my brain catches up, and everything snaps back into high definition. Sounds are clear, colors are sharp, and I remember who I am, magazine headline be damned.

I am Galen fucking Onasis.

I built my fortune from nothing.

I rule this company, and when I tell people to jump, they ask me: *how high?*

I am Galen Onasis, and my woman does not get cold, bruised knees, sucking my cock the first time we go further than a kiss.

Kara kneels for *no one*, and when I lunge forward and grip her waist, lifting her onto my desk, her squawk of complaint bounces off me like a pebble.

"Fuck. That."

Kara looks hurt for a split second, heat rushing to her cheeks, but I nudge her to lie back and stretch out on top of my mail. My hand is steady as it drags down the length of her body—over her throat, her chest, her belly—before I cup between her legs. Heat sears through her underwear.

*God.*

A glimpse of blue lace panties makes my lip curl, and I'm fucking savage, gripping Kara between the legs and kneading her with my palm.

"That is the last time you ever kneel on the floor. You hear me? You are a queen. You want something from me, you hop up on this desk and let me take care of you."

Kara's breathing is ragged, her frown fixed on the ceiling where sunlight spears through the skylights. She fiddles with the hem of her bunched up dress and rocks up against my palm.

"But what if I *want* to suck your cock?"

I grip her pussy tighter, my pulse pounding in my ears. "Then you will. But somewhere comfortable. Somewhere that no one could walk in."

"They could walk in now—"

"And see the boss worshiping you."

You know, it's a bit too fucking appealing when I say it like that. I wouldn't exactly mind if some of those managers who refuse to ask Kara questions came up here and found my tongue buried between her legs, her hair spilling out of her bun as she bucks and writhes on my desk.

"You want to risk it with me, Kara? You going to let me taste you?"

Her breath comes in shallow puffs.

And I wait, heart slamming against my rib cage, vibrating with tension until she licks her lips and whispers, "Yes."

# Kara

Obviously I've thought of this before, and not just the other day. More like hundreds, no, *thousands* of times. I've dreamed of this so many times, I get a flash of deja vu.

This head of thick brown hair between my bare thighs, threaded with silver; the rasp of Galen's constant five o'clock shadow against my sensitive skin. It's so familiar. And inevitable.

My boss yanks his chair over, then sits like a king at a feasting table. He's still cupping my pussy, holding me there as though if he lets go, I might float away.

*You are a queen.*

Shivers race over my body, because I'm goody-two-shoes Kara: eternal dork and known stick in the mud. No one has ever looked at me the way Galen Onasis looks at me.

Like he'll never get enough of the sight of me.

Like he resents needing to blink.

"I've thought about this so many times, Kara." His voice is

48

guttural.

"Same," I whisper, then break into giggles.

This is so strange.

The steady stroke of his free hand up and down my side—that settles me. Eases my building hysteria. Because what am I so nervous about? This is *Galen,* and we've both wanted this for so long, and I know down to the marrow of my bones that he would never, ever hurt me.

Piss me off? Sure.

Make the occasional—gasp—error in judgment? Of course. Despite the reputation he's cultivated, Galen Onasis is a human being. A flawed mortal just like the rest of us.

But even during our earlier mess, amid all the hurt feelings and confusion, I've always found solace in this: the look of adoration in his ice blue eyes. The edge of hunger that makes his handsome features so stark.

He won't care that my panties are frayed. Or that I, um, haven't shaved down there in a few days.

"I'm going to look at you now."

Jeez, I hope he doesn't narrate the whole experience. I'll embarrass myself, because every time Galen says things like that in his deep, rough voice, I almost burst into flames.

"Oh gosh." I cover my face with my hands, my own cheeks scorching against my palms, as Galen flips the skirt of my dress up onto my belly. A thumb hooks under my panties, and he pulls them aside in one deft motion.

Silence.

I peek through my fingers—and melt into the desk.

There's no need to worry. No need to panic, and I should have more faith, because Galen Onasis does *not* look put off by my personal grooming and frayed panties. Quite the opposite.

He's staring at my bared pussy like it's a miracle.

"Fuck," Galen mutters, and gives himself a tiny shake.

My feet find their way onto his strong thighs, and now I'm spread open for him, knees bent, utterly shameless under the blistering gaze of my boss. The penthouse office is sunlit and golden, and this is perfect, perfect, perfect.

"You're so fucking beautiful, Kara. Every inch."

My laugh sounds more like a wheeze. "You haven't *seen* every inch, Galen."

His smile punches me in the chest. "Yet."

Even as we speak, his thumb slides between my slippery folds. I'm so slick already, swollen and needy and wanting, and I might be embarrassed about that except Galen groans with delight.

His chair creaks, his body shifting, and then his hot breath wafts over my pussy. I bite down on my bottom lip—hard.

"Easy." With his free hand, Galen takes one of my tight fists and uncurls my stiff fingers. "We can stop anytime. Alright?"

Ha. "That's not the issue."

His thumb rubs circles into my palm. He's so patient with me. So kind. "Then what is?"

Well, since he asked... "The issue is that if I don't feel your mouth on me soon, I'm going to bite through my own tongue."

Galen's low chuckle vibrates the air near my clit—then he grips my hips, tugs me closer, and he's *there*. So hot, so wet, so demanding. Hungry licks and the rasp of his stubble.

It's so much to take in, and I'm spinning into the air, floating high above this desk on a happy, tingly cloud.

"Such a good girl, Kara." Oh god, I'm going to melt. I'm a shivering mess. "Fuck, you taste good. Look at you, rubbing yourself all over my chin, so needy and perfect. That's it, princess."

A finger circles my entrance as Galen laps at my clit. It eases inside me slowly, long and surprisingly thick. My gasp is loud in the quiet office, the only other sounds the creak of Galen's chair and the obscene wet noises coming from between my thighs.

Paper crinkles as I thrash around. Oh, shoot—his mail—

"Leave it," Galen growls, and I nod frantically, shoving my hands into his hair. He's right. Doesn't matter.

A second finger joins the first. I cry out, long and low, my back arching off the messy desk as I tug and twist his hair. The way those broad shoulders hunker over me—that freaking waistcoat—

"Galen," I whimper.

"I've got you." Thick fingers crook inside me, and I see stars. "Beautiful girl. Gorgeous girl."

When teeth scrape over my clit, my hips jerk. My breath seizes. And then lips seal over the tight bundle of nerves, sucking hard, tongue swirling, and I... and I...

"Fuck!" I curl up off the desk, chin to chest, shuddering as I come for what feels like an eternity. I'm pure liquid heat, every nerve in my body singing.

When I collapse back against the crumpled mail, Galen beams at me, his chin slick. "That's the first time I've ever heard you curse, Kara. What an honor."

And he's impossible, so infuriating sometimes, but I can't address that right now because there are more pressing problems. An urgent concern.

"Fuck me." Paper crinkles as I struggle to sit up, my movements still sluggish with pleasure. I tug at his shirt, his waistcoat, his collar. "Stand up and fuck me. Shoot, I can't reach your belt."

When Galen stands, he looms so much my chin tips back, my heart hammering. One strong hand rests on his belt buckle. "Are you sure? Someone could still walk in."

"I don't care." I really don't. I'm leaving this company anyway, right? Moving to a better position, yes, but also so that Galen and I have a chance at a real future. So the thought of someone walking in doesn't bother me like it should; in fact—god help me—the thought sends more heat barreling through me like a wildfire. "I want you, Galen. Want you inside me."

I don't need to ask a third time.

My boss yanks his belt open; unbuttons his pants with deft fingers. Pulls out his hard length, the skin ruddy and moisture beading the tip.

Can cocks be handsome? Because it's a very handsome cock, and it looks painfully, *viciously* hard.

"You haven't done this before." Galen states it as fact as he moves between my legs, even though I've never specifically told him that. But we've always been like this: communicating silently on our own private wavelength. The two of us against the world. "I'll go slowly, but tell me if it hurts too much. What we just did should help."

Yeah, yeah. I fix him with my sternest glare.

"Get inside me, Mr Onasis."

There's that grin again, and his cock nudges between my folds. He rubs it all the way up and down my slit, up and down, coating his shaft in slickness and teasing my clit. When he finally pauses at my entrance, my toes are curled behind his back and my stomach is tensed.

"Deep breath in." I fill my lungs obediently, eyes locked

on Galen's. He smiles, so full of love, the corners of his eyes crinkling. "And exhale."

As I breathe out, Galen presses forward, splitting me open.

# Galen

H eaven. I've never been a religious man, but Kara's
pussy makes a compelling argument that heaven
exists. She's so tight and hot, so wet and needy, her
inner muscles gripping at me and sucking me deeper.

"Alright?" I grit out, sweat beading on my spine beneath
my shirt. Next time we do this, I want us both naked. Skin
to skin. I squeeze her gorgeous, thick thighs, lifting them to
wrap around my waist. "Kara?"

"It's good." She sounds winded, her forehead pressed against
my shoulder. If I wasn't wearing this fucking shirt, I'd feel her
skin against mine. "Oh, gosh. So good."

We're back to *gosh* then—back to prim and proper. But I
swear to god, I will draw more curse words from her yet.

I feed her another inch.

Kara lets out a squeak.

"You feel so right." I'm not a chatty man usually, but with
my cock inside her, I can't stop talking. Can't stop this steam
of consciousness, this landslide of fervent praise. "Like you

were built for me. So fucking perfect. Yeah, grip me, princess. Squeeze me tighter."

Kara's pussy clamps around my cock, and I tip my head back, ears ringing, my laughter light. It's so damn sunny in here, like we're fucking above the clouds.

My girl grips two handfuls of my waistcoat, clinging tight. Her breaths come heavy as she presses her words against my throat. "Go—Galen. Go deeper."

Yes, ma'am.

It's the greatest privilege of my life to draw slowly out, then sink my shaft inside her. Deeper and deeper, in and out, on and on, until the desk rocks beneath us and Kara's rolling her hips, tilting to meet each thrust. Our hands are everywhere, roaming and greedy, and our breaths mingle as we kiss—draw back—kiss again.

I never dreamed I could get this lucky.

"You know how many times I thought of this?" My thrusts turn rougher, a little mean, but Kara doesn't mind. She lets out a moan, low and throaty, and rolls her hips to meet me. "You know many times I wanted to bend you over this fucking desk, princess? How many times I wanted to stretch you out on that conference table with everyone looking, so I could tear your shirt open and suck on these tits? God. You know how many times I nearly lifted your skirt and sank into you in the back of that fucking car?"

These aren't the right things to say. They're too raw, too primal.

Too honest.

And Kara deserves sweet things, gentlemanly things, but she turns me into a goddamn beast. I want her so badly. *Need* her so badly. Even right this second, with my cock buried inside her and her taste on my lips, it's not enough.

It will *never* be enough.

"Touch yourself." I know I should do it, but I'm a greedy man. I want to see how Kara likes it when she's alone. "Show me how you get yourself off."

Slender fingers swirl between us, her fingertips brushing against my plunging cock, and I tilt back, staring. Ruined. She's so neat and precise in her movement, even in this, and it's giving me heartburn.

Spasms flutter through her pussy. Kara grips me tighter, then lets out a whine. Her fingers circle faster, her breaths frantic.

"Do it," I grind out, fucking my assistant harder against the desk. "Do it, Kara. Come for me."

This is only the first time, I remind myself. It's the only way to fight back the panic; the wild urge to stop her, to drag it out longer, to make this last for days and weeks and months and years.

It's the first time I'm feeling her come. The first of many.

Kara's jaw clenches; her head tips back. Those eyes are screwed shut, and her soft, desperate noises are music to my ears.

When Kara falls apart, something shifts deep inside my chest. Locks into place. She's *mine,* and I'm hers. I already knew, of course, but now it's done. It's final.

I've been Kara's for a long, long time.

"Perfect," I mutter against her temple as she sags in my arms. So perfect.

Then I spill inside her, filling her up—and let every last doubt and fear wash away.

# Galen

\* \* \*

*Three years later*

The only warning I get is the hum of the elevator. The golden light begins to glow, racing through the floor numbers, and I lean back at my desk, steepling my fingers.

Only one person is brave enough to enter the penthouse of the Onasis Studios skyscraper without an invitation. Just like only one person makes my heart pound without trying.

We weren't scheduled to meet until lunch, and I planned to go to her, but my wife is less of a stickler for planners and appointments these days. Well... outside of work, anyway.

And it's been a long time since I was Kara's employer.

I do miss those days. But what we have now is much, much better.

It takes the elevator less than two minutes to climb the whole building, the silver box racing up to the clouds. That's two minutes to tug my tie straight; to drum my fingers on my desk.

Patience. Not my biggest virtue.

The doors hush open and the sight of her hits me like force field. It always does. Whether in her pajamas with no make-up, or in her heels and sleek dresses, my wife always short circuits my brain. Today, she's in a royal blue wrap dress, her dark hair swept over one shoulder.

"Quiet morning?" My voice carries between the olive trees in their planters, and Kara's steps are soft against the tiles. Since she started to show, she's swapped out her heels for ballet flats.

Thank god. I was fending off nightmares about twisted ankles.

She shrugs, strolling closer. "I'm the head of Strategy. I can step out and clear my head if I want to."

Fuck. Is that what she wants from me? A brainstorming session?

Or will she let my hungry mouth between those thighs?

"I brought you something." Fuck, I hadn't even noticed the bakery box she's got balanced on one palm. Kara sets it on my desk, and I'm already grinning.

Muffins—I know before she lifts the lid. We've always been two steps ahead, reading each other's minds, and muffins are our thing. Hey, there are worse mascots.

"I hope you don't bring your new boss any baked goods." I lift out the nearest one. It looks like salted caramel, and my stomach growls. Did I miss breakfast again?

Kara rolls her eyes, but she's smiling. "Hardly. And she's been my boss for three years, Galen. That's not new." She leans her hip against the desk, but I'm already pushing my chair back and patting my thigh.

My pregnant wife does not lean against that hard wood. She sits where she belongs: on me.

"You sound crazy," Kara says when I tell her that, but she settles on my thighs anyway, then reaches for a triple chocolate muffin. "One day your ego will land you in trouble, Galen Onasis."

I chuckle into her hair.

I deserve that—and I love her teasing. I love her prim little movements and her sexy as hell clothes. I love the vanilla scented candles she's scattered around our home, and the way she says *oh, gosh* when I thrust inside her.

"Take the morning off." My palm spreads over the firm curve of her belly, holding tight. "Stay with me a while."

Kara's head tips back against my shoulder. "You're not too busy?"

Never for her. I'm never anything less than thrilled to see Kara.

"I think you know the answer to that." And she does, because she's already squirming in my lap, her breaths getting choppy as I abandon my muffin to explore.

I'll finish it later.

First, I want something sweeter.

# II

## Sweet Tooth

# Description

I'm an ambitious lawyer. She's a cake pop delivery girl.

**I cannot *believe* they've made me her babysitter.**

After a decade of long hours and non-stop grind, I've been tapped to make partner. I'm so close, I can taste it. The only catch? First, I need to babysit our biggest client's niece while she launches her cake business in our building.

She thinks overworked lawyers are the perfect crowd for sprinkles and sugar. *I* think it's a waste of damn time.

But I've worked too hard for this promotion, and I will not let this girl derail me now. Not with her antics, or her cakes, or her teasing little smiles.

Yes, she's sweet and pretty. Yes, she makes my cold, dead heart race in my chest.

But she's a distraction. That's all.

# Julian

You know what it takes to be a lawyer? A *great* one? People think you need to argue well and bullshit even better–and sure, those are important skills, but they're not the magic ingredient. They won't get you a corner office on the top floor.

People think of sharp suits and buffed leather shoes and expensive haircuts, like you can win over a judge or jury simply by looking the part. And okay, there's some truth to that too.

People think lawyers need to be assholes. That you can't give a shit about the world. I say that's optional, but fine.

And people say you need to hold your liquor and schmooze your way around the city, taking cards and remembering names. Again, a kernel of truth, but that's not all.

The one skill you *really* need, that you won't last a day of law school without, let alone the job? You've got to thrive under pressure. You've got to see the work piling up and the deadlines coming in fast and the competition probing at your soft spots, and instead of panicking or daydreaming about buying a farm in the country or some shit, you've got to *smile*. Like you're on top of the fucking world.

It's a challenge, that's all. A chance to sharpen those teeth. A chance to show these other assholes that you're not to be trifled with.

And hardest of all, you've got to *mean* it. Can't fake low blood pressure–not for long. Either you're up to this, or you're not.

Anyway. I'm the biggest shark on the thirty-third floor, and the only way up from here is to make partner. I've got the big corner office and my own assistant. He screens my calls and waters my plants and makes me coffee from the machine the bosses gave me last year.

Vance and Irving both came down from the top floor and watched me drink the first cup, beaming with pride like they were watching their kid take his first driving lesson. It was weird, but I played along, toasting them both with a dark roast. Anything for the job. Thanks, dads!

I've come this far. Partner is so close I can *taste* it. I'm not going to fuck everything up now.

\* \* \*

"Rodriguez."

Vance corners me in the elevator first thing on Monday morning, mopping the top of his bald head with a silk handkerchief as the doors slide shut behind him. It's just the two of us and a delivery guy—some acne-spotted kid drowning in his uniform and clutching a stack of parcels to his skinny chest.

I check my watch discreetly. I'm early. This is fine.

"Morning, sir." I shift over, conceding a few inches of space.

I give him the perfect amount—enough to show deference, but not enough to imply fear. I've been playing this game for almost a decade now, and I'm good at it. The best. "You play golf on the weekend?"

Vance *always* plays golf on the weekend. Those clubs are an extension of his gnarled hands.

"A few rounds, a few rounds..." The boss is distracted. He scrubs the handkerchief over his face, then clears his throat, shooting me a glance. "Are you busy, Rodriguez? Can you spare a few minutes on the top floor?"

This is a trick question. If I say I'm busy, I'm blowing off the boss. Obvious error. If I say I'm free, he'll think I'm not pulling my weight.

"I can move some things around," I tell him smoothly. "I'll make it up over lunch. What do you need?"

Bingo. Vance shoots me a grateful smile, tucking his handkerchief away.

Don't let his sweet-old-man act fool you. Irving and Vance both shuffle around this building like friendly grandpas, practically digging in their pockets for boiled sweets for the interns, but they built this firm from nothing, and they have the hunting trophies to prove it.

Figuratively speaking. Hunting is too boisterous for these two, especially at their age. All I'm saying is they've buried a lot of competitors in their day. Their desk chairs could be piles of bones.

"We'll speak upstairs."

Okay. That's fine. Most information that passes through this building is sensitive in some way, and we don't want the delivery guy getting an earful. He's already tense enough, the tips of his big ears turning pink.

It's like he can sense he's stepped into the tiger cage. Smart kid.

The elevator climbs quickly, cold seeping through the external glass wall. The city skyline is dark against the sunrise, and thousands of lights are still on, winking gold from the high rises.

We let the delivery kid out on floor twenty seven.

"It's nothing," Vance says a moment later, even though I didn't ask. The elevator floor purrs beneath our feet. "Nothing to worry about, Julian."

Nothing to worry about?

And he's calling me by my first name?

Well, shit.

* * *

I get a two minute elevator ride and a brisk walk down a carpeted corridor before we push into one of the top floor meeting rooms. That's my shot to prepare. In that time, I've run through every case I've had for the last six months. Every interaction with a major player in the city.

There's nothing. I'm sure of it. I win my cases, and I bring this firm big money. I don't screw around with interns, and I pass on tips to the higher-ups. So why the hell have they pulled me up here on a Monday morning?

*Nothing to worry about*, Vance said. People don't say shit like that when they've got good news. That's what you say when you're trying to soften a blow. He leads me into the meeting room now, and Irving stands to greet us at the conference table. The sky is getting lighter behind him.

Two old lawyers. Vance is stocky; Irving is gaunt. Vance is

bald; Irving has a bristly mustache. Vance favors pinstripes, and Irving likes pale pink pocket squares.

That's it. Those are all the differences. But one big thing they have in common is the insistence on using a meeting room when they're both required to be present. God forbid one of them attend the other's office. It'd mean conceding ground.

So here we are, on neutral territory. I resist the urge to fiddle with my cuffs.

"What can I do for you, sirs?"

They like that. Vance and Irving share a conspiratorial smile, playing the misty-eyed fathers routine again. Give me a break.

None of us would be here if we weren't made of pure ambition.

They sit, so I sit. There's a jug of water, so I pour three glasses. Irving is slightly closer so I pass him a glass first, and Vance's eye twitches in response.

*Clink.* I set his down. He'll get over it.

Glasses delivered, I settle in my chair. From the outside, I know exactly how I look: relaxed. Confident. Pristinely dressed, with a charcoal waistcoat and burgundy tie. Bearded, yes, but it's a *trimmed* beard. No scruff in sight.

Inside, though, there's acid eating through my guts. I like pressure, yes, but not walking into a trap. I worked too hard in this firm. I don't want any damn curve balls, that's for sure.

"Julian." Vance says my name fondly. Irving bristles, annoyed that the other man's taken the lead. "You've worked here for how long now—six years?"

"Eight," I say. He knows that, the asshole, he's just trying to worry me. Trying to make me feel unnoticed and disposable to them. But two can play at that game, and I lean back with a broad smile. "Yes, it's rather a long time, isn't it?"

Read: I can walk any time I like, you wrinkly fuckers, and I'll take your bottom line with me. Don't try this shit on me.

Irving clears his throat. "Quite."

Vance's voice is cooler when he speaks again, but that's fine. Better that he's wary of me than taking me for granted. "You're due to make partner, of course. There's no one better for the honor. No lawyer more deserving in the building."

...Here we go.

"But?" I drum my fingers against the table, impatient for the punchline. This is not a celebratory conversation. This is a shakedown. "What's the catch, sir?"

Out comes the handkerchief again. He swabs at his forehead, then gestures for Irving to take over, face flushed.

The other man looks sour, but he picks up the thread. I'll remember that in the future–that Irving had the backbone, not Vance. "But we have a problem we'd like you to solve for us first. Or rather... there is a task. Of an unusual nature."

I roll my stiff neck, breathing in through my nose. An unusual task? That could be anything, and I won't react until I hear what it is.

Finally realizing that I don't plan on speaking just yet, Irving pushes on. He flattens his palms on the conference table, and his next words are stilted. Rehearsed. "Do you know the Briggs family, Julian?"

Obviously. "They're our biggest clients." They're old money–the kind of family that comes with an investment empire attached. Trust funds and charities. Prenups and divorce settlements. So many properties, they've probably forgotten about a few. The Briggs family could keep dozens of lawyers busy year-round.

Irving nods and pushes on, still talking like he's reading off a note card. "Well, the Briggs family has asked us for a small favor. Their business is very important to us, of course."

"Naturally."

"And this favor requires someone we trust."

So whatever it is, the bosses can't—or won't—do it. But they won't ship it out to just anyone, either, not when the stakes are so high.

I'm so fucking close to making partner. Once I land that promotion, I'll be on the fast track. More money, bigger clients, freedom from *this* type of bullshit. Then one day, once I've milked Irving & Vance for all the company's worth, I'll start my own firm—and I'll do it with a nice, long contact list and accolades to my name.

I tug my cuff straight. "What do you need, sirs?" I'll repeat the question until I'm blue in the face. They'll get tired of wasting time eventually.

And sure enough: "One of the Briggs girls—she's a fresh little thing, just turned twenty two. She's starting some kind of cake business, and she needs an office as a base."

"An office," I say flatly. "For cakes."

"To sell them, not bake them. Apparently she's pitching to the grab-and-go crowd. Hungry workers chained to their desks."

"Oh, you're using chains now?" I shift in my seat, gusting out a sigh. "What does this have to do with me?"

For two busy men, they're dragging their feet on this explanation. Not a good omen.

"Her family is… protective of this one. They want someone looking after her at all times."

"They want a babysitter," I translate, my mouth suddenly

bitter. Eight years of working here, for this? To become a glorified nanny to a spoiled rich girl?

"It's not for long," Vance breaks in, finding his tongue again at last. "Two weeks at most. This is a trial period—she'll use our firm as a base to test her products and prepare her business. Then she'll launch across the city and get out of our hair."

As one, Irving and I glance at the other man's bald head.

He scowls back at us, but for once, I don't care about soothing his ego.

I am a *lawyer.* A damn good one, too—the best in this building by far. I earned that partnership, and yet they're dangling it like a carrot, making me jump through this ridiculous hoop. Dios mío.

Enough messing around. "I want to make partner within three months."

"Done," Irving says quickly.

"Put that in writing and send me the full contract. The expected pay rise and bonus—everything. And I'll keep an eye on her, but that's it. I won't answer for whether her business flops or not, and I won't keep her *entertained.* I'm not taking her to the damn zoo."

Vance raises his palms. "It's barely anything, Julian. Escort her to and from the office each day. Keep an eye on her while she's here, and if she needs help or resources, lend her your assistant. Keep the Briggs girl happy."

Oliver is *my* assistant, damn it. He's an employee, not a stapler.

"Fine," I grit out. "Send the details over and have Oliver put her in my calendar."

"No need," Irving says. "You start tomorrow." I clench my jaw so hard my teeth ache.

Surely even *actual* babysitters get more warning than that.

# Lola

W hen the intercom buzzes, I'm shoving one arm into a brightly patterned shirt and clutching a poppy seed bagel in the other. My pink hair is damp from the shower, and I changed my outfit four times already this morning before settling on high-waisted black leggings and a baggy shirt knotted at the waist. Is that too casual for an office? Should I add a necktie?

*They're lawyers, Lola. Not the fashion police.*

Too late now, anyway. My stomach's still twisted up like a pretzel, and I'm breathless when I abandon my bagel and stumble to the intercom. "Hello?"

"Lola Briggs?" The tinny voice is deep. Crackling with static.

"That's me."

A heavy sigh gusts through the speakers. "Alright, then. Let's go."

That's it. No 'good morning'. No 'your ride is here'. Just: let's go. And let me tell you, *no one* talks to the Briggs family like that. My all-powerful uncle would chew them into pieces and spit them out if they did, and woe betide anyone who insults his precious Lola. I'm *delicate*, see?

Ugh. It's the worst.

But hearing someone address me like a normal girl, like a regular pain in the ass—it's a weird little thrill. I kinda like this intercom grump.

"I'll be right down."

My outfit may be a lost cause, but I *am* prepared. I stayed up past midnight last night, checking and rechecking my supplies, then stacking them carefully by the door. I've spent the last few days making lists and schedules and plans. I. Am. Ready.

My first day! So exciting.

Since spending the last decade shut away in sterile rooms and private hospitals, I never did that first-day-of-college thing. I didn't go to parties or dates or cookouts, and I was never a regular teenager. I barely saw further than my yellow bedroom walls. And I'm twenty-two now, but I'm still greener than grass. I only moved out on my own two weeks ago, striking out into the big, wide world.

So maybe the nerves fizzing in my belly are totally normal; maybe it's common for my hands to shake and for me to barely fumble my apartment door open. Maybe a normal girl would clatter down the staircase like a moving disaster zone too, dropping a trail of colored markers and tubs of glitter behind her.

A man stands in the center of my building's lobby, watching me come downstairs, his face carefully blank.

My sandal slips on the final step. I stumble forward, dropping a sheet of poster board with a smack. The man sighs.

"Miss Briggs." It's not a question. It's the sound of a man

resigned to his fate, and gosh, if someone handed me a pen and notepad and told me to draw a sexy lawyer, I'd definitely draw this guy. He's well muscled under his tailored clothes; he's tall and broad-shouldered. He looks expensive, like the human embodiment of fine brandy, with dark hair and smooth, light brown skin.

His scowl is harsh and his beard is sleek. Should I tell him I want to pet it?

Probably not.

A second man scurries across the lobby, and shoot, I didn't even see him standing back there. How could I when the scowling man takes up so much presence, like a black hole sucking all my attention? But this second guy darts me a smile, and he's way less intimidating. His suit is baggier, his chestnut curls flopping over his forehead, and freckles dust his pale cheeks.

"This is my assistant, Oliver. He'll help you in the office."

"Hi, Oliver. Thank you so much," I add, because the cutie's picking up my trail of debris from the stairs. I beam at him, and he blushes, fumbling my poster board.

Another deep sigh from the grump.

"Please be ready in the lobby at 7:30 sharp every morning."

I hitch several tote bags higher on my shoulder, the straps cutting into my collarbone. "Sure, okay. I'll be on time, I promise." He turns on his heel to leave, and I hurry after him. The street outside is cool, sunshine bathing the sidewalk, and pale white blossoms cling to a nearby tree.

"Um, sir?" He doesn't turn back, though I *know* he hears me. My sandals slap against the sidewalk as I chase him. "Sir? What should I call you?"

A small shrug. The grump leads us to a sleek black car,

pulling the rear door wide, and gestures inside at plush leather seats.

"Courtesy of your uncle," he tells me. Then to really hammer home what he thinks of me: "Most people would walk the nine blocks."

I huff and squeeze past him, tumbling onto the backseat in a landslide of boxes and tote bags. I may not be sick anymore, but I haven't regained my strength either. Nine blocks? I might as well run a marathon. I'd turn up then need a three hour nap, but there's no way I'm telling the grump that.

"You didn't answer my question," I prod instead. "What should I call you?" Because somehow, I don't think 'sexy lawyer' will go down well.

It's Oliver who squeezes into the backseat beside me, juggling my dropped poster board and glitter tubs. The other man shuts the door on us with a thump, then slides into the front beside the driver.

He turns to face us. Draws his dark gaze over me from head to toe, lingering on my pink hair and knotted shirt with flamingos printed on it. My muddle of craft supplies and tote bags. The car pulls into the street, the cool air con tickling my warm cheeks.

"What do you usually call your nannies, Miss Briggs?"

Oh. Oh, he's *such* a jerk. Oliver winces beside me, but I ball my hands in my lap and hit the grump with my sweetest, don't-give-a-damn smile. I haven't had a nanny for years, but sure, I had them before I got sick. They were awesome, too. They're *still* awesome, and they all keep in touch. They all come to Briggs family barbecues. "Their names, of course. So what's your name, please?"

Skyscrapers slide past the car windows.

"Mr Rodriguez," he finally says.

I turn to Oliver. "You don't get a 'mister'?" Out of the corner of my eye, his boss bristles. I guess I shouldn't ignore him in favor of his assistant. Too bad, so sad.

"Oliver is fine." His assistant's blue eyes dart between us, back and forth, back and forth. He looks fascinated—like he's watching a tennis match.

I nudge Oliver with my elbow. "So is Lola. We'll be spending a lot of time together, right?"

There's a muffled snarl from the front seat. Somehow, I don't think Mr Rodriguez is too excited to be on Lola duty, but hey—I'm not thrilled with him either. I glare at the back of his perfect head as we drift through lanes of traffic, at the dark hair curling against his neck. He's so *strong* looking. Like he's been sculpted from marble.

Well, the man's gorgeous, but he's an asshole. A grade A jerk.

With any luck, I'll spend the next two weeks with Oliver and barely see this guy.

* * *

"Oh, good." Four hours later, a rich drawl curls through the office. I stiffen where I'm sitting cross-legged against the wall opposite Oliver's desk, pieces of poster board splayed out around me like a glittery fall out zone. The door to Mr Rodiguez's office has opened, and he's leaning in the doorway. His jacket is gone, and his shirtsleeves are rolled to the elbow. His forearms are corded with muscle where they cross over his chest. "It's arts and crafts hour. My favorite part of daycare."

Why? Why did I do this to myself? Why did I bring a bunch of crap into this office to *draw*? This idea made so much more sense in my head, damn it. Sure, I came up with a bunch of logo designs on my own, but I wanted to play-test them. See how people responded to each one, then tweak in real time.

The end result? Day one, and I look like a crazy person. And I've spilled glitter *everywhere.*

"I'm working on logos," I tell Mr Rodriguez from behind the pink curtain of my hair. If I don't look at him, maybe he can't hurt me. Like a bogeyman. "To see which one customers like better."

He hums. "And busy lawyers are the perfect judges of design."

"They're my target audience," I say, though it sounds weak to my own ears. God, can I even do this? Starting a business is a really big step. It took me over an hour last night to order groceries. I kept getting overwhelmed and closing the website tab.

"You could have brought completed designs."

Yes. Yes, I could have. But I didn't do that, because I'm an idiot.

I blow out a shaky breath, and my poster boards blur in front of my watery eyes. Steps drum across the carpet, then buffed black leather shoes stop beside my crossed legs.

"Sprinkletown." Mr Rodriguez says it the same way he might say 'garbage patch'. This close, I catch the faint scent of his cologne–he smells warm and expensive and masculine.

Well, I guess two out of three isn't bad.

"You don't like the name?" I croak.

He hums, noncommittal.

"I like it," Oliver volunteers.

Thank god for sweet assistants. I shoot Oliver a grateful smile, and he jolts with concern at my damp eyes and blotchy cheeks. He opens his mouth to say something, but I shake my head quickly.

*Please, no. Please don't give your boss anymore ammunition.*

"Sprinkletown cupcakes," Mr Rodriguez drawls.

"Cake pops," I correct. "They're like lollipops, but, um, made of cake. They're more portable and less messy. Better for office workers."

A black shoe scuffs at the glitter now ingrained in the carpet. "Yes. In offices, we do hate mess."

"Sorry." Curled up on the floor, I feel about two inches tall. Like I'm shrinking down to live in the carpet like a flea. A glittery, fabulous flea. "I'll clean it up before I leave."

There's a grunt, and then he strides away, thank god. Off to bother Oliver about meetings and memos and other lawyer stuff. They mention a court date and my ears perk up—gosh, I watched so many legal dramas on the hospital wards—but I know better than to ask. Halfway into my first day, and my survival instincts have finally kicked in.

I sniffle quietly, tugging my favorite logo closer. This one, I think. This is the one I'll take to the break rooms for feedback.

\* \* \*

Uncle Ray calls when we're in the car on the way home. Mr Rodriguez is in the front seat again, paging through a stack of papers on his lap, while Oliver types like crazy on his phone. They're definitely heading back to the office after this, and jeez, how late do they work? It's 5pm and I'm so tired, I'm a zombie. If I stayed out another minute, I'd start walking into walls.

"Hey, Uncle Ray." In the front seat, Mr Rodriguez stiffens.

He stops shuffling his papers, blatantly eavesdropping, and usually I might take this chance to mess with him, but tonight, I'm too tired. "What's up?"

"Hey, Lola-Rose." He calls me that, even though it's not my name. Says it's because I'm pretty as a flower. All at once, homesickness slams into my chest so hard I can barely breathe.

There's no one waiting for me at home, not like when I lived on the Briggs family estate. No sweet uncles or aunts or cousins; just my dark, empty apartment, the silence so thick I can hear my own heartbeat.

"How was your first day? Were the lawyers nice to you?"

I stare at the back of Mr Rodriguez's head. He's so freaking obvious, listening in like that, but I don't want to argue with him. I don't want anything except maybe to lie my head in Aunt Hattie's lap and feel her stroke my hair while I fall asleep.

"It was good, thanks." My voice is small, so I clear my throat. Try to sound convincing. "I picked out a logo. And we settled on Sprinkletown."

"That's great, honey!" I slam my eyes shut, swallowing past the lump in my throat. What is wrong with me? Must be hormones or something. "And they were nice to you?" he asks again.

"They were nice," I whisper. Then cough, and speak louder. "Super nice. I–I worked with this guy Oliver today. He's the best. He's sitting right here, riding home with me."

I don't mention Mr Rodriguez, but I don't call him a jerk either. I'm not out to cause anyone trouble, and next to me, Oliver nudges me with a goofy smile.

"Good," Uncle Ray says, and he sounds relieved. "And you're not too tired? You don't feel dizzy? Don't forget, you can take as many days off as you need."

"I will," I say, even though I don't plan on slacking off. Everyone else may think this business is a hobby, a phase I'm going through, but I *really* want it to work. Can't make that happen by babying myself, can I? "Thanks for checking in, Uncle Ray."

"Any time, Lola-Rose."

I stare out of the window the rest of the way home.

Tomorrow will be better—that's what I always say. It's the mantra that got me through those hospital checks and rounds of treatment; it reminds me to think of bright, happy things.

Tomorrow will be better, and Sprinkletown cake pops will be awesome.

Mr Rodriguez will see.

# Julian

Day two of Lola-sitting, and I offer to fetch her alone. It's hardly a two man job, and this way my assistant can get a start on his day. On *our* day. But Oliver guffaws loudly at the offer and drops his briefcase on the desk, then turns on his heel and leads me to the elevator.

"That's not a good idea, Mr Rodriguez."

I follow, mouth pressed in a flat line. Why did I make such a point of telling Oliver he could challenge me whenever he liked? That I value his input? Clearly that was a mistake.

"Why not? It's nine blocks and a ditsy girl with pink hair. I think I can handle her."

Oliver jabs the elevator button and throws me a look over his shoulder. "That's what I'm afraid of. You already made her cry once, and I'm not going to watch you ruin your career just because you're pissy about Lola being here. I don't want to work for these other lawyers, Mr Rodriguez. They're boring."

"I did not make her cry." I step inside the elevator beside Oliver, glaring at the shorter man. I did *not* do that. I think I would have fucking noticed.

Noticed, and gone easier on her. I'm an asshole but not a monster.

"She cleaned the carpet," Oliver says. "The glitter's almost gone."

I huff. "She did not cry."

"I saw her." He frowns at the panel of floor buttons, watching them light up one by one as we descend. "When you were bitching at her about arts and crafts."

Oh, come on. That was ridiculous. Who brings glitter tubs and poster board to a professional office? Who wears flamingo printed shirts and dyes their hair pink? This is a law firm, not a festival ground.

"I do not *bitch*."

The look Oliver levels at me speaks a thousand words. I grunt, tugging my jacket sleeves straight.

Maybe I was harsh. I certainly didn't get this far in life by rolling over and showing my belly–I've fought tooth and nail for every victory. And there are days when this place feels more like a battleground than a law firm.

Maybe I should lower my weapons. At least with Miss Briggs.

After all, I don't come after Oliver like a snarling tiger, and he's the best assistant I've ever had. There's something to be said for that trust, the camaraderie that comes from *not* trying to one up each other and stab each other in the back all the time.

What is this? Is Oliver using this as a teachable moment?

I watch him out of the corner of my eye. My assistant is wearing a salmon pink shirt today, and it matches the constant flush on his cheeks. "Are you managing me again?"

"Yes," he says simply, smiling brightly as we step into the Irving & Vance lobby. Our shoes echo against the marble tiles, and through the glass doors, the car service idles by the sidewalk. "You can thank me later, Mr Rodriguez."

I should ship this kid back to HR.

\* \* \*

Nine blocks is a ridiculous distance to order a car service, especially since the morning traffic is almost as slow as walking. Who is she, royalty? When we step out onto the sidewalk at her building, the vicious comments are already lined up on my tongue. I swallow them back, the cool morning breeze ruffling my hair. The street smells like asphalt and ozone.

Maybe Oliver's right. Maybe I was too hard on Lola. I fiddle with my collar, annoyed, as we step into the lobby.

I fully expect her to run late. For us to buzz the intercom again, and then to watch her clatter down the stairs with another armful of ridiculous supplies. Finger paints, maybe, or a tie-dying kit.

Instead, Lola's waiting in the lobby with a single cardboard box in her arms. She's dressed more demurely today, in a gray button down shirt tucked into black pants, and she looks tired. Dark shadows cling to her eyes, and her lips are pale.

Her hair's still pink, thank god. But drawn back in a low bun.

"Miss Briggs." There's an uncomfortable tug in my chest as I take her in. "You're on time. Good."

She nods, but she won't meet my eye—though she smiles at Oliver as she trails past. He offers to take the box from her arms and she refuses politely, leading us out onto the sidewalk.

Where the hell is Lola Briggs, and who is this tired, sad, monochromatic girl? Where did all that color and life go? She was only with us for one day!

Fuck. I really am a monster.

Oliver beats me to the car, so he gets to open the door for her. She smiles again and thanks him, settling herself gingerly on the back seat. Is she in pain? What is happening here?

I slide into the back seat before Oliver has a chance. There's a huff of laughter, and then the door closes behind me with a thump.

Lola glances over, and jerks when she finds me instead of Oliver. I don't examine the bitter possessiveness that snakes through me at that. Is my assistant really so much better? He's friendly, yes, but like a golden retriever. Bouncy and often irritating.

"Oh. Um. Good morning, Mr Rodriguez."

"Good morning, Miss Briggs." I scan her from up close, then peer into her cardboard box. Lola flips the lid shut, her lips pursed.

Oliver climbs in beside the driver, and we pull away, then coast through the morning traffic, the car silent and sleek. The driver's listening to the radio, the news bulletin almost impossibly quiet, and Oliver chats with him about some college football game.

I stare at the shadows under Lola's eyes. "Did you sleep well?"

She peeks at me, then away. Frowns out of the window, her pulse tapping in her throat. "I slept fine, thank you."

Liar. "You look tired."

Lola scoffs. I wait, but apparently that's all she's giving me.

A scoff. What does that *mean*?

"No arts and crafts today?"

Her mouth twists, but she says nothing.

"You did a good job with the carpet," I offer.

Lola nods, still staring out of the window instead of at me. "Maybe I'll open a cleaning business instead of Sprinkletown."

"That's a pity. It's a good name."

Finally, she looks at me. Steals a glance to check whether I'm mocking her or if I mean it. And I mean it, okay? I thought about it a lot last night. The name grew on me... and so did Lola.

Fuck, did I really make her cry? I haven't felt this shitty since I yelled at Oliver for spilling coffee on my case notes.

Oliver forgave me, though, especially after I apologized loudly to him in the break room, then offered him a long weekend to go visit his parents. So maybe Lola's not a lost cause either.

"You don't need to worry, Mr Rodriguez." Hope bubbles up inside me just in time to be popped. "I won't get you fired, and we can spend the next two weeks staying as far away from each other as possible. Maybe tomorrow, Oliver could fetch me alone."

She thinks I'm groveling for my job? Hell no. Julian Rodriguez does not crawl for anything, and he certainly doesn't beg little girls not to run to their big, scary uncle. Who the fuck does she think she's dealing with? How does my career hang on this stupid situation? Why does she want to be alone with Oliver so badly?

Resentment simmers in me, toxic and hot.

"That's good," I say, and I can't stop the vicious words as they punch out of me. Somewhere in the back of my head, the conscience that sounds suspiciously like Oliver screams at me to stop talking. "I would hate for you to cause more trouble than you're worth, Miss Briggs. God forbid you waste anyone's time. But hey, you have a powerful uncle, right? So I suppose that makes *you* worthwhile. Oliver and I would be lucky to kiss your feet."

No sandals today, I note. No sparkly blue toe nails. Plain black ballet flats.

All at once, I deflate. Regret is sour in my mouth.

I've done it again. Taken my frustrations with Irving & Vance out on this girl—who already looks like she's weathered a few blows today, and it's not even 8am. Her shoulders curled over as I talked, and now she looks even smaller, lost in the wasteland of plush black leather car seats.

My chest throbs.

"Listen, Lola—"

Her fingers tighten on the box until the cardboard creaks. Her voice is a whisper. "Please don't."

Ah, shit. I feel like something sticky on her shoe. Her sensible, tragic little shoe.

Outside the car, the buildings sliding past are familiar. We're nearing the office, and *no*, I can't let her scurry away from me like this, all hurt and rumpled and small.

"I'm sorry," I say quickly, wincing as I sense Oliver stop chatting to listen in. "That was uncalled for, Miss Briggs. I am a little... frustrated by our current situation, but it's nothing you've done. Forgive me. Oliver can tell you—I am not a morning person."

"He's not," Oliver choruses helpfully from the front seat. "One time I brought him a breakfast muffin and he tossed it in the garbage."

Lola's eyebrows flick up.

"It smelled like death," I tell her. I won't be unfairly maligned. "Truly awful. And he smeared ketchup on my office door handle."

Oliver snorts, and Lola's lips twitch, and my heart thumps harder in response. It feels like victory. Like winning a case in court. I grin at her and she smiles back, shy and unsure.

I'll take it. God, I'll take it. Not because I'm scared of her damn uncle, but because I hate seeing this girl hurt. And I hate even worse knowing that I'm the asshole responsible.

"All meat smells like death if you think about it," my assistant muses. When the car slows outside the office, I leap out and beat Oliver to Lola's door, holding it open for her and avoiding his eye.

His knowing gaze still makes the back of my neck itch all the way up to the office.

It's a relief to shut myself away and leave the two of them out there together.

## Lola

❦

Oliver connects my laptop to the internet and gets me settled on the end of his desk. It's a large table, all glass and chrome, and I wince as my rolling chair squeaks with every movement. My cardboard box is tucked away by my feet.

"Are you sure I'm not bothering you here?"

Oliver shakes his head, scrolling through Mr Rodriguez's calendar. Even with my partial view of the screen, I can see his boss is a very busy man.

A busy, bad-tempered… sometimes sweet man. A powerful man who knows how to apologize. Seriously! I thought those were a myth.

"Don't worry about it, Lola. It's nice to have some company here besides his Highness."

I hide my smile behind my hand, clicking away at my own screen. Pulling up the detailed customer survey I compiled last week.

Okay.

Okay.

I check my email. Send off a photo of my chosen logo mock-up to the graphic designer I picked out. Check the news. Look up nearby noodle bars for lunch.

But finally, I can't escape reality anymore. The whole reason I'm *here* instead of working at home on my sofa is so I can do market research. So I can trial designs and flavors and ideas, and eventually, force feed these lawyers free samples.

Oliver chuckles when I collapse on the desk, face squished against my folded arms. How can I go out there and talk to all those serious, professional people? What if they all hate me like Mr Rodriguez? "Feeling shy of the scary lawyers?"

I nod, bun wobbling. "Uh-huh. I need to ask them to fill out a survey."

"Don't worry. They won't bite."

I puff out a breath. A strand of my hair keeps sticking to the corner of my mouth. "Because of my uncle," I say flatly, the words echoing weirdly against the glass table. Isn't that what Mr Rodriguez implied this morning? That my presence here is a pain, and not a freely given favor like Uncle Ray told me? So humiliating.

"Well," Oliver says. "Yeah." My heart sinks to somewhere near my toes, but Oliver shoves his chair back. "Come on, I'll go with you. Mr Rodriguez can answer his own calls for an hour or two."

The last thing I need is more reasons for that man to hate me... but the temptation of company is too much to resist.

"We'll go to the break rooms." Oliver tugs me to my feet. "We won't be interrupting anyone there. And shit, people love talking about food, Lola. Plus these are some of the most opinionated assholes you'll ever find." I trail him to the printer against the wall, jabbing at buttons until warm white copies of my survey start spitting out into the tray.

Oliver sucks in a deep breath, waving a hand by his face like a sommelier. "God, yeah. I love the smell of toner in the morning."

I bark out a loud laugh, glancing nervously at Mr Rodriguez's closed door. Behind the polished wood, his deep voice rumbles as he talks on the phone.

"He said he likes the name Sprinkletown."

Oliver's grin is wider than the Cheshire cat's. "Oh, yeah. I bet he does."

\* \* \*

Two hours and eighty three completed surveys later, Oliver and I step out of the elevator, laughing. It's been so *nice* hearing people say they like my idea. That it's the kind of sweet treat they might actually buy. Not everyone said that, obviously, but enough did that I feel like less of an idiot.

And maybe this could work. Maybe it's not a crazy whim like everyone thinks. Because this is only one office building, but there are so many more out there. In this block, this postcode, this *city*. If I could sell my cake pops in even a few of those places, if I could get the Sprinkletown name out there, maybe...

Maybe I could build something all by myself. Could actually make something of my sheltered life.

Mr Rodriguez is waiting in his open doorway. He's scowling at Oliver's empty desk, but he transfers that stink-eye to us when he hears us coming.

God, he looks angry. And tall. And hot. His dark eyes sear into me, and goosebumps prickle over my skin.

"Where have you two been?" he grits out.

I wave my clipboard at him, completed surveys fluttering. "I asked Oliver to help me with these. I'm sorry I took him away from his work." No way am I letting Oliver take the fall for this one—he made going into all those break rooms so much easier. It's like he has a superpower for handling grumpy lawyers.

Mr Rodriguez snaps his fingers, then gestures for my clipboard. I carry it over to him, choking back a laugh. "Oh my god. Are you one of those people who click their fingers at servers?"

He takes my clipboard. Flips through the papers with a frown. "Of course not. What is this?"

"A survey. About cake pops."

Brown eyes flick to me, then back down. After a second, I remember to breathe again. "Naturally." Then the world tilts on its axis, because Mr Rodriguez draws a pen from his pocket and starts ticking boxes on a fresh sheet.

"Um."

He ignores me, scrawling a detailed answer to one of my questions.

"Don't worry," Oliver calls. "I'll help you read his shitty handwriting."

The frown deepens, but Mr Rodriguez keeps writing. Determined not to stare at his cheekbones like a weirdo, I read the bronze plaque on his office door.

*Julian Rodriguez.*

"I like the name Julian." Another fleeting glance leaves me tingling.

"And I like Sprinkletown." Lord, his voice is deep. Rich and smooth, like melted chocolate. "So I suppose we're even."

This is so different compared to yesterday. Compared to

93

frosty, pointed silences and his black leather shoe scraping my glitter over the carpet. I can't help beaming at him, practically bouncing on my toes, and when Mr Rodriguez hands back my clipboard, he looks a little alarmed.

"Get some work done, Oliver," he clips over my shoulder, then to me: "If you need anything else, knock on my door, Miss Briggs." He shoots a final sour look at his chuckling assistant, then shuts the door gently in my face.

*  *  *

"Be honest with me. How late do you two work?"

It's just past 5pm, and we're stepping out into the street. It's a warm evening, the sky's still light, and music floats out from a nearby bar. The sidewalk is thick with pedestrians running past in two streams, and I hurry after Mr Rodriguez as he cuts a path to the car, my box balanced under one of his toned arms.

"I'll get out of here in an hour or so," Oliver calls from a few steps back. *"That* guy probably sleeps at his desk."

Mr Rodriguez pulls the car door open for me and doesn't deign to snipe back at his assistant. But when Oliver tries to slide in beside me, a big hand clamps on his shoulder and steers him to the front of the car.

I watch Mr Rodriguez settle in the car beside me, butterflies dancing in my belly. He glances over, and seems relieved when I offer him a smile.

"I don't sleep at my desk," he says after a long moment, when the car pulls away. His legs are so long, folded in the back like this. He must have been more comfortable when he sat in the front. "But Oliver can't imagine my existence when he's not there."

I bite the inside of my cheek. These two are such an odd pair.

"It must be lonely for him," his assistant sighs, shaking his head. His chestnut curls flutter in the air con. "So cold and gray."

Mr Rodriguez's eyes crinkle when he sees my lips twitch. And I'm filing all this away, rewriting the story of this man in my head to someone who lets his assistant sass him freely. Who's grumpy and strict and demanding, yes, but who has a sense of humor too.

He's downright indulgent with Oliver, though his assistant can only be five or so years younger. What must that be like—being one of Julian Rodriguez's soft spots?

A wave of longing crashes over me, and an ache throbs in my chest.

Just imagine it. God.

# Julian

After a week of Lola-sitting, I'm... acclimatized. It's automatic, when I arrive in the office on Monday, to drop my briefcase on my desk then march Oliver down to the car service, sweeping out into the traffic and crossing the nine blocks to her door. I haven't suggested again that he leave me to fetch her alone, and he hasn't offered.

Would Lola like that? Would it make her uncomfortable? Is Oliver protecting her from me? She hasn't been so tense around me lately, but god knows we got off on the wrong foot.

Fuck, I hate that idea. That Lola might find me frightening.

It's strange, because in my work, having a fearsome reputation can only be a good thing. I *want* my competitors—and some of my colleagues, too—to get sweaty palms at the thought of facing me. I've taken great care over the years to establish myself as merciless. A cold-hearted bastard with a killer instinct.

But I sure as hell don't want Lola to think of me like that. The thought makes my throat tight.

"Free samples this week." Oliver is practically giddy with glee, his knee jiggling as we share the back seat. "I asked Lola for double chocolate."

I resist the urge to cuff the back of his head. "You shouldn't give her extra work." She looked tired enough on Friday night after four full days at the office. After more market research and web design and all the exhausting nuts and bolts of starting a business. She was pale and gaunt, collapsing into the car service with a sigh of relief, her slender body drowning in another soulless button down shirt and sensible dark pants.

I did that. I stomped the color out of her on her first day.

What I wouldn't give to see that flamingo-print blouse again. We only have one more week to make that dream come true.

"It's not extra work," Oliver huffs. "I'm an office worker who loves sugar and snack foods that come on sticks. I'm her target demographic, and *I* love double chocolate. We don't all subsist on push ups and repression," he adds quietly, and maybe I really will smack him.

Oliver slides into the front seat while I meet Lola in the lobby. Her building is large and grand, my footsteps echoing off polished tiles, and she holds her palms up as soon as she sees me.

"Please don't be mad."

See what I mean? There's a lot I need to fix between Lola and I. She's squirming with anxiety as I come closer, my hands tucked in my pockets as I survey the giant suitcase at her side. Though she's dressed in gray and black again, her luggage is pure Lola. It's candy pink, with turquoise zips and handles.

Seeing that case is like finding water in the desert.

"Nice case." I grab the handle and start rolling it toward the street. Lola scurries after me, her pink head bobbing in the corner of my eye.

"I'm sorry it's so huge, Mr Rodriguez."

"Julian," I tell her.

"It's just, I wanted to bring enough samples to go around the whole building. To be efficient, you know? Then I'll be out of your way sooner."

My grip tightens on the suitcase handle. I keep my gaze fixed on the car waiting for us in the street. "There's no need to rush."

Lord, please don't let her rush. I want the full two weeks with Lola, and not a day less. She could move her whole apartment into my office and I'd still feel the same.

I roll her suitcase out of the lobby and across the sidewalk, leaning over to pop the trunk of the car. It takes me a minute to wedge the case inside–it really is a beast–and when I slam the trunk shut, Lola is still there. Watching me with those big, blue eyes.

I grin, rounding the car. "You couldn't open your own door?"

A few days ago, there would have been an edge to those words, and Lola would have flinched, a blush climbing her throat.

This morning, she laughs, waiting for me to hold the door open before sliding inside. Her body passes close to mine, separated only by a hunk of metal, and I catch a whiff of her vanilla scent.

"I like when you do it," Lola murmurs before ducking inside the car.

I stand on the sidewalk for a long moment, heart hammering. Did she really say that?

Jesus.

Once we're all folded inside the car, I clear my throat, thumb tapping against my knee. We pull into traffic, slow and easy. She likes when I do it? When I hold the car door? What else would she like me to do for her? Images batter my brain—a slideshow of carrying things for Lola and winding a scarf around her neck and fuck, lifting her up to see a high shelf—when Oliver pipes up from the front seat.

"Did you bring double chocolate ones?"

Ugh.

I slide lower in my seat and stare out of the window, face hot.

\* \* \*

Lola props the suitcase against the wall opposite Oliver's desk. I should go inside my own office and tackle the landslide of work waiting for me there, but instead I linger, peering over Lola's shoulder. She's kneeling, the lid of the suitcase flipped open, inspecting the dozens of clear plastic containers filled with cake pops for signs of damage.

"You baked a lot this weekend."

"Uh-huh." Lola lifts a box of samples from the back row. They're pink with sprinkles.

"Make sure you take some breaks. You look a little tired." God, this is like Oliver's first week as my assistant. He accused me of trying to baby him, and I scoffed and offered him a game of catch. But Lola's not offended, thank god, because she sits back on her heels and offers me a sunny smile.

"Don't worry, Mr Rodriguez."

"Julian."

A huffed laugh. "Don't worry, Julian. I'm just trying to cram as much into my time here as possible. I'll take a few days off before I launch for real."

I hope so. And I hope I'm around for that somehow. Will she sell her treats in this building? Or will she be sick of us by then?

If she takes her business elsewhere, will she stay in touch? Two weeks never felt so damn short.

"It's not long, is it?" Lola says quietly, and I guess we were thinking similar things. "I'm trying to cram a whole self-taught Business 101 course into a couple of weeks, but god knows if I'm on the right track. Most days I feel like a kindergartner pasting stuff to her head."

I hate the defeated slump to her shoulders. "You'll figure it out. You're a smart girl."

Lola smiles up at me again then, and too late, I realize how we're positioned—with me looming over her, and Lola on her knees at my feet. Blood pounds in my temples, and...elsewhere in my body, and I crouch quickly, bringing myself down to her level.

Behind us, Oliver taps away at his keyboard, gusting out one of the heavy sighs he saves for Mondays.

Lola makes a little squeak when I pluck her hand, wrapping it in both of mine. She seems flustered but pleased, and I hold her hand close to my chest. Oliver stops typing, but I don't care.

It's the first time we've touched. The first time I've felt her slender fingers, her pulse thrumming beneath the thin skin of her wrist.

"You're very warm," Lola murmurs.

Yes, that happens around her.

"You can do this, Lola." I squeeze her hand gently, and watch her shy smile bloom in response. "You can overcome any setback, and you *will* make Sprinkletown a success. I have faith in you," I add quietly, squeezing her hand one more time before I let it go.

When I push to my feet, Oliver's gaze makes my neck itch. I can't look at him, or Lola, or anything except my office door.

"Don't disturb me this morning," I clip out, striding to the safety of my office.

I close the door on their replies.

\* \* \*

It's 4pm, and I've had no samples. I want a cake pop, damn it, but I made such a stupid fuss about being left in my fortress of solitude that of course Lola didn't bring me one. Should I go poking around the break rooms? Or maybe Oliver has some on his desk. I pace up and down beside the glass wall of my office, the late afternoon sunshine warm on my cheeks.

Before Lola came here, I was so obsessed with my work that sometimes I'd forget to eat. I was a machine, a deadly, relentless machine, and my competitors had to live with the knowledge that while they were eating or sleeping or tending to their pathetic bodily needs, I was coming for them.

I'm not anymore.

Or rather, I *am*—I'm still doing my damn work. I'm still one of the best. But I'm not obsessed like I was, not single-minded in my pursuit.

Not with the law, anyway.

"Double chocolate," I mutter, tugging at my collar. I'm in a waistcoat and shirt, my sleeves rolled to the elbow, and the tie is the next to go. I can barely fucking breathe with Lola in this building, especially with this stupid scrap of silk choking me to death.

Oliver requested a flavor from her. I bet he got the first samples too. They're *close*, chatting all day out there, and lord knows she's spent far more time with him than with me. He's nearer her age, too.

…Does she like him? Does Lola have a crush on my assistant?

I snarl, tugging at my tie and working the knot tighter. I'm so busy growling and pacing and yanking at my clothes that I don't even hear the door nudge open behind me.

"Um." I whirl around and find Lola staring, wide-eyed. There's a tray balanced on her palms, with cake pops spread over white china plates. "Is this a bad time? Should I…" she trails off, blinking at the tie yanked part way around my throat.

Then she breathes out a laugh, and sets her tray down on top of a cabinet.

Lola approaches me like I'm a wild animal caught in a snare. I suppose she's not wrong.

"I always thought lawyers were so clever," my maddening girl says, plucking my tie out of my grip and working the knot loose. She's so fucking close, I can see each dark, curling eyelash; can see the delicate blue veins beneath her skin of her wrists.

When Lola shakes her head, biting back a smile, her pink ponytail rustles. Vanilla washes over me.

"This is no good." I slide her hair tie out before she can stop me, her strands silky against my knuckles. Pink waves fall to her shoulders, and Lola gazes up at me, breath held. Now we're even, freeing each other from these binds. "Pretty hair like yours should be loose. You wore it down on your first day."

Lola shrugs, but her cheeks are flushed as she goes back to

fiddling with my tie. "I'm trying to look professional."

"Well, stop it." I pinch the collar of her gray shirt and give it a tug. "I miss the flamingos. All those bright colors. Please, Lola, I can't go on."

"So dramatic," she murmurs, and my necktie slithers through my collar. She pulls it out slowly, the motion tugging me gently toward her. "Are you like this in court, Julian?"

"Of course." Her hips fit my palms so neatly. Lola doesn't push me away, not even when I step so close our chests brush. "When in doubt, strip. They teach that in the final year of law school."

Her laugh puffs warm against my throat. I squeeze her hips, biting back a groan.

"I brought you samples," Lola whispers.

"In a moment." God, I'd eat anything she brought me. Anything at all. But for now, I have my hands on her, and I've been waiting for this since the moment we met. She's *here*, pressed so close, gazing up at me with such trust, and the only thing I want to swallow whole is Lola Briggs.

But first: "What do you think of Oliver?"

She blinks, confused. "Oh, um. Your assistant? He's—he's nice—"

I swoop down and claim her mouth, chest rioting. She doesn't want him, which means there's still a chance that one day she'll want *me*. Julian Rodriguez, the declawed tiger. I kiss her like I'm stating my case, like I'm presenting exhibit A for why she should consider keeping me.

Lola sucks in a shocked breath, but then she grips my shoulders. Kisses me back. Her body bows against mine, every point of contact scorching through my clothes, and her mouth is hot, her lips soft, her breaths shallow.

I trail my palms up her waist, her ribs, her arms. When I trace my thumbs up her throat, her pulse pounds beneath her pale skin.

"Lola," I murmur against her mouth.

Her whimper is so sweet, I have to kiss it away.

Fuck. Kissing her… it's like nothing else in the world. It crackles up the length of my spine. I feel it in the roots of my hair.

We don't break apart until there are voices outside the open doorway. Oliver greets someone loudly—one of the bosses, by the sound of it, and Lola and I spring apart, smoothing our clothes and staring at the next room.

"Shit. I need—"

"It's fine," she says quickly, hurrying to the cabinet and rescuing her tray. "You can try them another day."

No!

Jesus Christ. So close to a cake pop. My stomach twists, miserably empty, but I scrub a hand over my jaw. Watching the flash of pink hair as she leaves, the jagged pieces inside me settle.

It's okay. It's okay. I'll try one soon.

Today, I tasted something much sweeter.

# Lola

You don't get much chance for romance on hospital wards. Kisses are the last thing on anyone's minds when you're surrounded by all those pale linoleum corridors and bright lights and beeping machines, so I passed my teenage years with zero experience. Untouched and unwanted—in that way, anyway.

When I was seventeen or so, I had this all-consuming crush on one of my doctors. He was Canadian, with this floppy blond hair, and he looked like he'd wandered out of a music video. But when I finally confessed my love to him during an appointment, he patted my hand, said 'thank you, Lola', then practically sprinted out into the hallway. He always brought a nurse with him to see me after that.

Talk about embarrassing. What was I thinking, telling a fully grown man that I wanted him?

I may be an adult now, but honestly, up until yesterday, I'd filed my fixation on Julian Rodriguez under the same category. The never-gonna-happen box. The you're-kidding-yourself-

Lola file. The just-buy-a-vibrator-damn-it section.

I mean, he's a lawyer. A grumpy, scary, freaking *gorgeous* lawyer in his thirties, who has a fancy office and can grow a proper beard. And me? I dragged a suitcase around yesterday filled with hundreds of cake pops. I spilled glitter on his office carpet.

Sure, I got all flushed and tingly from pretty much the moment I met Julian, but I never dreamed that he might want *me.* Half the time, I still feel like that awkward girl on the ward. The one that people only spoke to in hushed tones.

But Julian's never been careful with me—not in that stifling way. And lord knows he didn't go easy on me to begin with.

He's softer with me now, but it doesn't feel like pity.

It's because he wants me. He really does.

It was all in that kiss.

* * *

"Good morning, sunshine." Oliver beams as he walks into my building's lobby, spreading his arms wide like we've been apart for weeks, not hours. The street is sunny behind him, and Oliver's dressed in a crisp white shirt. "The boss had to take a call, so we're riding solo this morning."

I nod and force a smile, dragging another suitcase of samples across the tiles. Oliver takes the handle neatly, leading me out onto the sidewalk. "Some of these have my name on them, Lola."

I hum in agreement, following him out into the cool breeze, but I can't think straight. Julian's not here? Did he really have a call, or is he avoiding me?

Oh, god. He's like that Canadian doctor, sprinting away

down the hospital hallway. I feel sick.

"You should give Mr Rodriguez a cake pop today." Oliver pops the trunk, heaving the suitcase inside with far less grace than Julian did. The car dips beneath the weight. "He was such a bitch when he didn't get one yesterday."

So is that it? He's mad that I didn't give him samples? Except no, I *did* bring him a tray, and he spent that time kissing me instead.

Cradling my jaw and sliding his tongue into my mouth; nipping my bottom lip and growling low in his chest. Pressing his hard body against me.

Oh, god. My head spins as I topple into the back seat. I'm not equipped for any of this. Oliver slides in beside me, closing the door with a thump, then starts chatting happily as we pull away from the sidewalk. After a minute he eyes me carefully, then clearly realizes that I'm barely listening, because he leans forward and mutters to the driver instead.

Julian's not here. He's *always* here.

He kissed me yesterday, and now he's stayed away. Is that a coincidence? Or does he regret it already?

\* \* \*

Julian really is on the phone. He's been talking for *hours,* his deep voice rumbling through his closed office door all morning. Even from the next room, you can hear the impatient edge to his voice—and who can blame him? He must be thirsty. Must want to stretch his legs and find something to eat.

So he's grumpy. I shiver, though my skin is hot under my clothes.

My nerves aside, I like when Julian is grumpy.

I took a risk today. After he pleaded with me to bring the color back, I stuffed the boring, drab clothes from last week to the back of my closet. This morning I'm back in my leggings and sandals and another baggy, bright shirt knotted at the waist. This one is light blue with a watermelon pattern.

"I'm gonna do it," I tell Oliver. "If he throws his pens at me, I'll toss a cake pop in his lap."

Oliver snorts. "You're a brave soul."

It's not *really* scary going in to see Julian. I fix him a plate with a powdered cake pop and make him a coffee with the fancy machine, then fumble his door open with my elbow.

Julian spins around in his desk chair with a scowl.

When he sees my bright shirt, his scowl melts and his gaze heats.

"Yes," Julian snaps down the phone. "We've been over this. It's not admissible in court." His eyes follow me as I nudge the door closed with my hip, then pad across his room.

Jeez, he looks good today. Like a man in a cologne advert, but gruffer. Real. Flesh and blood and a crisp, tailored shirt, watching me come closer like a cat watches a mouse. He grits something else down the phone, some annoyed legal jargon, and I set the coffee and plate on his desk.

"A snack," I whisper.

"At last. My fucking cake pop," he hisses back, and my cheeks ache, I'm grinning so hard. This is the part where I should leave—where I should go take my samples round the building and leave Julian in here to get some work done.

I don't turn to leave.

Julian's hand finds my hip. He kneads me, his thumb digging into my tight muscles through my leggings.

"Well tell her the offer expires tonight. She can cover her

losses, or she can go down with the rest of them."

With a tug, I'm drawn down onto Julian's lap.

I've stared at his thighs a *lot* over the last week. At all of his body, really. And I knew, somehow, that they'd be rock hard and sculpted. I shift against his leg, trying to get comfy, gripping the desk for balance.

Muffled words float down the phone.

"No shit," Julian barks. "Life's not fair. I'm a lawyer, not a fairy godmother. I hope you're not relying on my bleeding heart. At least make this interesting for me."

Ha. He's kind of a jerk when he's doing the lawyer thing. Scratch that—he's a jerk when he does lots of things, but not to me.

As if he can hear my thoughts, Julian wraps an arm around my waist, tugging me close until my back presses against his chest. He rests his chin on my shoulder with a quiet sigh. Like I'm a comfort.

The voice ranting down the phone sounds tinny. Super boring.

I play with the strip of Julian's wrist peeking from his cuff. It's so solid and broad. Dark hairs dust his golden brown skin, and tendons shift as his thumb moves, stroking my belly. When I shift, it slips under my shirt and finds bare skin.

God. I could purr right now. I squeeze my legs together, all tingly and restless. Julian grunts, then sets the phone down on the desk and presses a button to put it on speaker.

"The date is non-negotiable." Julian watches me carefully as he nudges me to my feet. I step between his thighs, turning so my ass rests against the edge of the desk. He lounges in his chair, dragging his gaze from my bare painted toes all the way up to my loose pink waves.

"Be reasonable, Mr Rodriguez. That is not enough time to prepare." The voice behind me makes me jump. I forgot I can hear it all now—and they can hear me. I press my lips together, staring into fierce brown eyes.

"But it is enough." Julian smooths his palms up my outer thighs, my hips, my waist. He's mapping me, heavy eyebrows pinched in a scowl, and it's so freaking *possessive*—like he owns me. "Our team can manage it. Why can't yours?"

I clench my thighs again, choking back a whimper.

Julian smirks.

A sigh rattles down the phone. "We're making no headway here."

Julian tugs on the knotted ends of my shirt. "I disagree." The sides come loose, held together only by two buttons. Julian flicks them open, holding my gaze.

I want to giggle. Want to moan, want to gasp, want to say *something,* but I can't. All I can do is grip the desk tight and watch as Julian opens my shirt, his hot gaze licking over my bare skin like a tongue.

My belly button. My stomach rising and falling with each breath. The lilac lace of my bralette—Julian soaks it all up like it's the best thing he's ever seen. When he flattens a palm on my body, fingers spreading wide, it's like he's marking me. Locking me to his fingerprints.

He doesn't seem to care at all about the angry voice on the phone, or his assistant sitting just outside that door, or anything except leaning forward and pressing his bearded cheek to the bare skin of my chest.

"Vanilla," he murmurs.

"What?" says the voice.

"Nothing," Julian snaps. He grips the sides of my waist,

holding me close. It's like he's listening to my heartbeat, but that can't be difficult. My heart's pounding so loud, even I can hear it. "Do you have anything useful to give me today, or is your whole plan simply to waste my time until you've run out the clock?"

There's an outraged huff, and then the line goes dead. My penned up giggles explode out of me, and Julian leans back and chuckles, one thumb rubbing the lace above my nipple. I suck in a breath, arching into his touch. "Honestly, these lawyers have such thin skins. They're exhausting, Lola."

I weave my fingers through his dark hair. "Tell me about it."

Our kiss is fierce. Hot and demanding, all teeth and tongues. Any doubts I had this morning are long gone—he wants me as badly as ever. Worse, even, and when I come up for air, the sight of his arousal pressing against his fly makes my breath stutter.

"Your coffee will go cold."

Julian cups my breast again, kneading harder. "I don't care."

I rock my hips against nothing, whimpering when he pinches my hard nipple. "Ungrateful jerk."

God. He's hot and big and muscled and bossy. He's *everywhere*, invading all of my senses. Julian growls and surges closer, desk chair creaking, trapping me between his thighs—and I'm so caught up in the moment that I don't notice the plate sliding until it's too late.

*Thump.* It bounces, thank god, but powdered sugar explodes across the carpet. Julian and I stare down at the mess, his grip still tight on my waist, and a muscle leaps in his jaw.

For a horrible moment, I think he might yell at me.

Then: "Shit." His forehead thumps against my collarbone. "Lola, Lola. Beautiful Lola. Destroyer of carpets. When will I get you alone?"

The planes of his back are toned and broad beneath his shirt. His warmth seeps through the fabric, and I rub soothing circles over his shoulder blades, my insides all jelly. "Um. Well, you know where I live."

Is that desperate? Do I sound needy? God, I don't know, but Julian seems pleased with my answer. He nods once, brisk, then lets me go. Pushes to his feet and stares down at the powdered sugar on his floor.

"I'll clean it," I say quickly, but he's already waving a hand.

"Don't worry. It was my fault."

"But I—"

"Go take your samples around," he says, tucking a lock of pink hair behind my ear. His mouth quirks up. "Time for Sprinkletown."

I smile, but there's a sharp ache in my gut. I *hate* leaving him, hate retying my shirt and stepping out of that office back into reality.

Oliver raises an eyebrow at me, but I march to my suitcase, avoiding his eye and fighting the urge to smooth down my hair.

I'm not gonna start any rumors about Julian. Lord knows I've caused enough trouble.

# Julian

Once again, I am the only soul at Irving & Vance not to taste one of Lola's sweet little cake pops. I've tasted other things, of course—her lips, her sugared breath, her warm, bare skin—but still. It rankles.

I shouldn't go to her apartment. It's late, and she needs rest, but I've denied myself all pleasures for so long that our kiss has opened my flood gates. I'm weakened. Desperate for more. My system is overwhelmed.

I curse my own name, standing on the sidewalk and staring at her buzzer. It's old fashioned, made of bronze. Her place is very nice, as befits the Briggs family fortune.

Lola's first apartment is more expensive than any I could afford, even now. Even with a steep pay rise and fat bonus coming my way.

One day. One day, every block in this city will be open to me, and men like Lola's Uncle Ray will beg for me to represent them. Maybe I will, maybe I won't. It'll be for me to decide.

I blow out a harsh breath and press Lola's buzzer. She's on

the top floor—naturally.

"Hello?" She sounds sleepy, like I caught her napping on the sofa. Is she wearing pajamas? Does she have those pillow creases on her cheek? I check my watch: it's 9pm.

"Hello, Lola."

Her gasp crackles through the bronze grate. Then there's a loud buzz, and I push through to the lobby with a savage grin.

She let me in so quickly. Like she's as eager for this as I am. I'll reward her for that.

It's dark in here, lit by dim sconces on the wall, and the post boxes lining one wall are made of the same bronze as the buzzer. My feet drum against the tiles, and then I'm pounding up the staircase, my palm sweeping up the banister.

I've never come this far before. There are only four floors, but it feels like an age before I crest the top step. Stars wink through a large glass window in one wall, and an abandoned pink marker lays in one corner. I scoop it up, brushing off the dust. When Lola's door swings open, I hold it out like an offering.

"A casualty of last week, I think."

Lola takes the marker from me, cheeks burning. "I wish you'd forget that."

"Never, darling." Forget the first time I laid eyes on Lola? It'd be easier to forget my own name.

Plus, this way I can tease her, can work that adorable flush onto her cheeks. I follow her inside.

This feels so instinctive. Second nature, like of *course* I'd appear at her door late in the evening. Of course she'd lead me inside, even though she's barefoot with only tiny black shorts and a green tank top covering her up. Lola takes me to a small kitchen with high ceilings and a breakfast bar, and nods at a stool.

"Coffee? Or something stronger?"

No, she's not surprised to see me at all. After all, she practically invited me here earlier. *Well, you know where I live,* she said. Fuck, it's been bouncing around my skull ever since.

"Do you live alone?" I ignore her offer for now. If there's a chance at all of my touching her, I want her clear-headed and enthusiastic. But if there isn't, then yes, I'd like to drink my feelings, please. Lola shrugs one shoulder, wrapping her arms around her waist.

"It's a family apartment. Obviously. My cousins stay here when they have business in the city sometimes, but yes, it's just me right now."

"You don't seem very at home."

Lola smirks, but there's no humor in it. "It's lonely. I'm used to my uncle's estate, with family around me all the time. And before that, even the hospital wards were—" She breaks off abruptly, frowning at the floor. "I, um. Can we forget I said that? I didn't want to tell you about that just yet."

I nod, though my chest aches. She was ill? Why doesn't she want to tell me? Maybe I do want that drink. "Then I didn't hear it."

A relieved breath. "Thanks."

We wait. A clock ticks in another room, and traffic rumbles past down below on the street. And when Lola speaks, she sounds so bitter. "It doesn't matter, does it? You already see me differently. Poor sick little Lola."

She looks tired again. Tired of the world.

"No." I slide off my stool, stalking closer. She shakes her head as I get near, glaring at a spot on my shoulder, and she looks so good in the soft lamplight. Like something from a dream.

"I'm healthy now, okay? Can't that be enough?"

"It is." I take her hips and pull her flush against my body. Grind my cock against her, because sometimes actions speak louder than words. "Does this feel like I'm worried you'll break?"

As fast as her anger came, she softens again, her forehead dropping to rest against my chest. Two arms snake around my waist, and she's rocking against me too. Clenching two fistfuls of my suit jacket and trying to squeeze us impossibly tighter.

She feels it too. This unstoppable draw between us. The primal need to get closer, to swallow each other whole.

"Lola," I groan. Her hair smells so good. "Do you know why I came here?" She shakes her head, still rocking against me. "Little liar."

That earns me a laugh, and I drag my chin over the top of her head, my beard rasping against her pink waves. "I came to lick your pussy, Lola. Would you like that?"

There's a squeak, but she doesn't sound horrified. She rubs her hips harder against me, her hot breaths seeping through my shirt.

"Is that a yes? I need the words, darling."

"Such a lawyer," she huffs. "*Yes.*"

\* \* \*

"Lie back on the bed."

Lola crawls onto the mattress, her hands and knees sinking into the plush white covers. Her tiny shorts cling to her peachy

116

little ass, and I watch it sway with my jaw clenched.

"You're so bossy, Julian."

I tilt my head, standing a few feet away. My hands are tucked loosely in my pockets and my shoulders are relaxed, but inside, my heart is pounding. "I thought you liked that." She certainly blushes when she hears me giving orders in the office.

The sheets rustle as Lola makes herself comfortable, and I take a moment to peer around her bedroom. It's a large white room, with one door to an en suite and another to a walk-in closet. Floor-length white drapes cover huge glass windows, and a thick sage green rug covers most of the floorboards. It smells like fresh linen and chamomile.

There's a king sized bed, two nightstands, a laptop glowing on an armchair.

No other signs of life.

You can tell Lola hasn't lived here long purely by the lack of color, and suddenly I'd pay good money to see her *last* bedroom. To see what she hung on the walls, and which vibrant shades she splashed everywhere. To smell her scented candles.

The brightest pop of color in *this* room is her pink hair, splayed over her pillows.

Lola stares at me, eyes bright and lips parting. Her finger draws gentle circles on her stomach. "Are you just gonna stand there?"

I bite out a laugh. "No." My shoes land on the rug, and the bed dips under my weight as I crawl over the mattress. I prowl up the length of Lola's body, until my face hovers above hers and my hands are braced by her shoulders.

She twitches when I brush a kiss to her throat, and I press my question into her heated skin. "Is that how it is? Are you going to be a brat, darling?"

Tentative arms wind around my neck. "It works for Oliver."

A laugh rumbles through my chest into hers, and I sink a little lower. Feel the softness of her body against my hard, unforgiving one. The dips and swells of her curves. "Believe me, Lola, I like you a lot more than I like him."

When I lift my head, she looks so fucking pleased.

God. I'm addicted to this woman. All I've done is crawl on top of her, and already I'm giddy with her. Intoxicated by her heat, her scent, her smile. I kiss her roughly, slanting our mouths together, and it's self-preservation. I need her just as lost to this as I am.

Lola squirms beneath me. She presses her soft tits against my chest; hooks an ankle over my calf. She's rubbing and panting and whimpering for me, and fuck, this is better than any triumph in court.

"Up." I ease back and lift her tank top over her head, tossing it onto the rug and following it with her bra. When Lola flops back against the sheets, her nipples are hard and rosy in the cool bedroom.

I duck my head. Lap at one with my tongue, then the other, and all the while Lola tugs at my hair and moans.

She's so sweet. Like sugar dusts her skin. Her fingers scrabble at my collar, but I shift out of reach.

"No, I think I'll stay dressed tonight, Lola." There's something so pleasing about the image of her sprawled out and naked for me, while I loom over her in a shirt and waistcoat and tie. Something so decadent and depraved. And she gets it, because she blushes even harder and whimpers, then helps me wriggle her shorts and panties down her thighs.

Of course, there are drawbacks to my plan. When I trail

kisses down her writhing body, pausing to suck a bruise on her hip bone, when I dip my tongue into her cute belly button, my cock aches from pressing into my fly, and there's no relief.

At least when I lie between her spread thighs, I can rock my hips into the mattress, and though it hurts, it's a good kind of hurt.

Just like my feelings for this girl.

"Lola." Her thigh muscles jump and shudder under my palms. I rub smoothing trails over them, up and down. And there, so close she must feel my heavy breaths, is her slick, swollen pussy. "Lola, darling, you're ever so wet."

It's obvious even without touching her. Her inner thighs are shiny with it, and the air is laden with her sweet, musky scent. A growl rises in my throat and I lunge forward, licking a stripe up her seam.

Lola gasps, hips rocking up to meet my tongue.

"Good girl," I grate out. She whimpers again. "Fuck, you're sweet. Who needs cake pops when I can eat this cunt?"

Her giggles fade into moans. And I'm feverish with her, with her taste and her needy sounds. I lick her until my jaw aches; I slide one then two fingers inside her, pumping them over her sensitive inner walls. I knead her soft tit, pinching and plucking her hard nipple, and every gasp, every cry, is music to my hind brain.

*Mine.*

Lola is mine. I want to keep her.

"Julian."

She's panting. Hanging onto my hair for dear life, yanking and twisting at the dark strands, and I stop sucking on her clit long enough to tell her, "Don't make me bald, Lola. I don't think you'd like me as much without hair."

A gentle kick to my ass. "I *would*. Oh my god, oh my god—"
I like to pretend that she's praying to me.

Because it's been torture, having her so near in the office and not being able to touch her. Not being able to taste. And sitting in the backseat of that car together, her vanilla scent in my lungs, feeling her warmth *right there* and yet keeping my hands to myself?

Pure torment. I pay some of that torment back now, tenfold.

I draw my spare hand down and gently spank her pussy. I shove her thigh over my shoulder and shove my face deeper, replacing my fingers with my tongue. I *own* her body, inside and out, and when I slide two fingers back inside her, Lola is hoarse with begging.

"Come on, Lola," I coax, fingers pumping in and out, my hips rocking against the bed. "Flood my tongue. Give it up, mi amor." I suck her clit into my mouth one more time and she arches off the bed, stiff and shuddering. Her pussy clamps down on my fingers, waves pulsing through her body, and her breath seizes.

She's so perfect. Fuck, I almost can't stand it.

Lola lets out a strangled cry, then flops back onto the mattress. Sated. Damp with sweat. I extricate myself as gently as I can, drawing my fingers out and sucking them clean, and she's salty and sweet. I'm already hooked on her taste.

Heavy-lidded eyes watch me, lost in a chaotic mound of pillows. "I can't believe you kept your clothes on. You're such a deviant, Julian."

I snort. If only she knew *half* the things I wanted to do with her. But hey—she'll find out in good time.

"I'm your deviant." I crawl up to lay beside her, and my cock is throbbing against my fly, but I don't care. I won't rush her.

I won't be the villain everyone thinks I am. A cynical part of me waits for Lola to send me away now that her curiosity has been sated, now that she's successfully hunted the office tiger, but she just rolls over and cuddles into my chest, flicking at my shirt buttons.

Sweet relief.

"I *will* get you naked sometime."

I grin at the ceiling. "Excellent. I look forward to it."

"So you…" Lola's voice is halting. She buries closer into my neck. "You'll want to do that again?"

Ah, I see. We're afraid of the same thing. Of making ourselves vulnerable and only getting one taste before being tossed aside. Forgotten.

That would never happen to Lola. Not with me around, anyway, so I roll over without warning, caging her in my arms. "You are *mine,* Lola Briggs." I nip the tip of her nose, and she giggles, relaxing already. "Of course I want to do that again."

# Lola

~~~
I float into the lobby on a cloud. Julian's already here, lounging against the bronze post boxes in a tailored navy suit, and he straightens when he sees me, his dark gaze scorching me as I hop down the last few stairs. His chest expands as he takes in my flippy yellow dress, patterned with daisies.

"Fuck," Julian mutters.

Good. I hoped he'd like it.

He takes my hand as we walk out to the car, and I dart a glance at the front seat, but it's empty. "Oliver finally left you alone with me, huh?"

Julian smirks and opens the rear door wide. "No suitcase today?"

"Nope." The cool leather brushes against my bare legs as I slide in. "I'm getting a bunch of cake pops delivered by a local bakery that I've sent my recipes, and then I'm selling them in a nearby investment firm this afternoon as a trial run. My uncle set it up."

I wait for Julian to say something sarcastic about how Uncle Ray keeps paving the way, but he doesn't. He just smiles at me, eyes crinkling. "Good."

Neither of us point out that I don't really need to be at Irving & Vance today. I could've had the cake pops delivered to my apartment, but then I'd have missed *this*. My morning ride with Julian. Stolen moments with him at the office. I couldn't stay away.

Three more days. It's Wednesday today, and Julian will be done with Lola-sitting by Friday night. My chest throbs.

I hate the thought of not seeing my grumpy lawyer every day.

The car drifts through morning traffic, the driver's window cracked and the radio humming, and I shoot Julian a nervous smile. He frowns, looks like he's about to say something, but then his phone rings. He pulls it out with a muttered curse. "Excuse me, Lola."

This is what it would be like, I guess—our time together. Julian's a busy man. A high-powered lawyer, and that comes with long hours and lots of urgent phone calls. Is that something I want to be around? Uncle Ray was barely home when I was a kid.

I sink back against the seat, mouth twisting.

Reality is such a bitch.

He's still on the phone when we pull up outside the office. I open my own door before he can reach it, hopping out onto the sidewalk. Julian rounds the car, and he gives me a rueful look as we enter the lobby.

He doesn't take my hand again. I guess he can't.

He barks something down the phone. He sounds grumpy.

The elevator doors sweep open, and we crowd in with a

few interns and a delivery man. Julian and I stand at the back together, a muffled voice floating out of the phone held to his ear, and as we swoop up the floors, he switches the phone to his other hand.

His knuckles brush mine. My stomach flips.

"No," Julian clips out. "That is unacceptable."

I wrap my whole hand around one of his long fingers, clinging on for dear life, and we ride to the thirty third floor like that, our secret contact hidden behind the wall of interns. When we step out onto our hallway, Julian smiles at me briefly, then tucks his hand in his pocket.

Yeah, no kidding. I'm not gonna paw at him in front of Oliver. The fact that he thinks I would pisses me off, and I stomp after him down the hallway. Jeez. I'm not *that* clueless.

I'm still grouchy an hour later when the cake pops arrive, but the scents of warm sponge and sugary frosting chase all my troubles away. They're spread out in long, flat white boxes, shiny and perfect and bright. Strawberry and vanilla and chocolate and toffee, dipped in chopped nuts or pretty sprinkles.

"Oh, wow," I breathe.

Oliver clatters over to stand at my shoulder. "Holy shit," he says. "Those look legit."

I pluck out a double chocolate cake pop and push the stick into his hand. "Try one. Go on, tell me what you think."

"I already tried the samples," Oliver argues, but he's staring at his chocolate cake pop with pure lust.

"These are fresh, though, and warm, and a proper bakery made them. They used my recipe, but still. It's gonna be way better."

The cake pops even *look* better. Neater and evenly sized. My mouth waters just staring at them.

Oliver sinks his teeth in with a groan. His eyes practically cross, and he holds up his thumb. I beam at him, heart light.

This is gonna work! It *is*. With a lot of help from Oliver and Uncle Ray and even Julian, sure, but it will work. Sprinkletown is go.

"I'll take them right over. I want the finance people to smell them while they're warm."

Oliver leads me to the elevator and presses the button. "You're devious, Lola.  Mr Rodriguez had better watch out—he's not the only one with the killer instinct."

\* \* \*

After hours of carrying a heavy box of cake pops up and down a skyscraper, I am *tired*. My arms feel like limp noodles, and my sandals drag against the sidewalk as I make my way back to Irving & Vance. I need a glass of water, a banana and a nap, in that order.

It worked, though.  My body may be wrecked by today's work, but my brain is lit up and sparking.  I beam as I cross the lobby to the elevator, my dress swishing around my thighs. The last few cake pops shift in the box, scraping over the glossy cardboard, but it's much lighter now.

They *sold*. People loved them. Wow.

It's amazing. The best day ever, and all I want to do is tell Julian about it. I slump against the elevator wall, the floors swooping past, and picture his expression. He'll be so proud.

Oliver's not at his desk when I reach our floor, so I shuffle right past and thump Julian's door with my elbow. He calls out in his low voice, and I fumble the handle down then step inside.

He spins to face me in his chair.

I hold my box up. "Special delivery."

When Julian brightens, I can't believe I was ever afraid of this man. He's a teddy bear masquerading as a scary lawyer, and when he pats his thigh, I kick the door shut and practically skip over, exhaustion forgotten.

I set the box carefully on his desk—no more carpet disasters—then sink onto Julian's lap. He sweeps my hair over one shoulder, pressing kisses to my neck.

"I thought you were desperate for a cake pop."

Julian snorts and wraps a possessive arm around my waist. "I'm desperate for *something*. This dress is cruel, Lola. An act of aggression. You're trying to give me a heart attack at work."

I hum, kicking my heels. "Oliver did say I have killer instinct."

"He's right." Long, elegant fingers gather my dress slowly up my thighs. I puff out a laugh and lean back against his chest, legs inching wider.

Julian doesn't touch me yet, though. He traces maddening circles on my inner thighs, but he murmurs in my ear. "You were annoyed at me this morning. For talking on the phone."

I bite my lip. Busted.

"I'm working on my grumpy reputation so we can match," I say, trying to joke it away. Because it seems so petty now, hours later. So embarrassing.

But Julian squeezes me, not buying it. "Lola. Tell me."

And there's nothing for it except to screw my eyes shut and force out the words. "I just—all I wanted as a little girl was my Uncle Ray's attention. And he was always too busy, taking calls or having meetings or drinking whiskey in his study with

126

other powerful men. Sometimes it felt like he barely even noticed me before I got sick. And I know that I'm not a kid anymore and you don't owe me anything, but I…"

Julian licks my pulse point. "You want my full attention."

I choke out a laugh. It sounds so dumb. "Yeah. I guess so." And I wholly expect him to laugh it off too or even be annoyed, but Julian rumbles with dark satisfaction. Like he *loves* hearing how bad I've got it for him. How possessive I am with every scrap of his time.

"I would like the same."

I splutter, feet swinging. "Yeah?"

"Yes. I'm jealous of your cake pops." Those teasing circles on my thighs creep closer to my center, closer to the pink lace of my panties and the aching, needy part of me behind them. "I won't take them away, of course, because they are important to you. But I would like it stated on the record that I'd prefer to be the center of your world."

I frown at his darkened laptop screen. "Are you making fun of me?"

I can't tell anymore, but Julian growls and nips my earlobe. "No. I'm explaining to you that my work is important and I cannot neglect it, but I understand your frustrations because I feel them too. And I hope we can find a balance together, because if there's one thing you can be sure of, Lola, it's that you are *always* on my mind. Day and night. Here and everywhere else. Okay, mi amor?"

Yes.

Yes, it makes sense, and it's so okay that I can't stop smiling. I flip the cake pop box open and drag it closer. "Which flavor?"

Julian sucks in a ragged breath, burying his face in my hair. "Vanilla, of course."

I lift the last vanilla cake pop out, passing him the stick. It's dipped in white chocolate and covered with pink sprinkles. His dark eyes bore into me as he takes his first bite.

"Delicious," Julian rasps, licking a stray crumb off his bottom lip, and god, I can't take it anymore. His sharp jaw and those cheekbones—that beard and his soulful eyes. I slide off his lap onto the floor, kneeling between his spread legs, half hidden under the shelter of his desk.

Julian watches me tug his belt open with a strained expression, then sets his half-finished cake pop on the desk. "I can't eat while you do this, Lola. It's too much, even for me."

I laugh, his zipper crackling as I tug it down. When I draw out his cock, it's thick and warm in my hand. He's already hard, his shaft pulsing under my fingers when I squeeze it gently, and Julian spreads his legs wider and lounges in his desk chair like a king.

Long fingers spear through my loose hair. "Lick the tip, Lola. Treat it like another cake pop—but watch your teeth." Julian chuckles at his own joke, rolling his neck. "There's my good girl."

Flames lick at my insides, and I shift on my knees. What is it about Julian calling me a good girl that makes me so freaking wet? And he *knows* it too, the bastard, because he's watching me with primal satisfaction etched on his handsome face.

Last night, he buried his face in my pussy like he wanted to drown in there, and I try to bring the same fervor now. I work the base of his cock with my hands, gripping and twisting, and run my tongue over every bare inch of skin.

I rain kisses over him.

I suckle on the tip.

I slurp him all the way down, as far as my throat will allow.

"Yes," Julian hisses, the chair squeaking as his hips buck. "Fuck, Lola. Your mouth. Your pretty mouth."

I hum, and I'm rewarded with a ragged groan. He strokes my hair and pulls on the strands; he scratches my scalp and rubs my earlobes between finger and thumb. Julian can't stop *touching* me, his cock thrusting carefully past my lips, and I can smell him. He's soap and salt and fine cologne. A faint undercurrent of musk. Freaking delicious. And he's hot, too, his cock so hot under my hands, his thighs bracketing me with firm warmth, and I've never felt so surrounded.

"Look at you." Each word grinds out of his chest. "Look at you taking me so deep. The *sounds* you make, Lola."

I hum again, and he thrusts harder. Hits the back of my throat and makes my eyes tear, but I moan loudly. I want him losing control; I *like* him coming undone.

"Lola, my Lola."

We're so lost in Julian's muttered curses and my moans and the creaking chair that we don't hear the office door open. We don't hear anything, until my Uncle Ray bellows and charges across the office. "Lola-Rose! Get *off* her."

He drags me out from under the desk by the elbow, and Julian jerks back and stuffs his cock away. I bang my knee on the table leg as I emerge, pain radiating through the bone.

By the doorway, the two old lawyers from the top floor crowd inside with a white-faced Oliver.

"Uncle Ray!" I yank my arm free, cheeks burning and eyes damp. Of *course* this would happen during my first blow job—I'd have an accidental audience of judgy old men. Fuck my life. "You should've knocked!"

My uncle gapes at me, turning crimson to his thinning gray hair. "This is an office," he bellows. "These people are at work,

Lola. *You* might be playing make-believe at having a job, but that asshole knows better!" He jabs a finger at Julian over my shoulder, but my ears are ringing. My chest feels raw.

That's what he thinks I'm doing. Playing make-believe.

…Is he right?

I wrap my arms around my waist, face numb.

"Don't speak to her like that," Julian's saying somewhere behind me, his voice muffled. Uncle Ray yells something in return, but I don't hear it. I don't hear any of it.

"It's not Julian's fault," I rasp. "I—I came on to him."

"He knows better."

"He's right," Julian snarls. "I should've known to lock the fucking door."

The older lawyers are arguing now too. Everyone's yelling except Oliver, who stares at me with shock and pity. He jerks his chin at the doorway, and I stumble forward, relieved.

It's cool in our—his office. Somehow I don't think I'll be invited back. And it's quiet, except for the muffled yelling and the *click* as Oliver picks up his desk phone.

"They're hypocrites," he mutters, stabbing at the buttons as he dials. "Show me any powerful man in this city and I'll show you someone who's hooked up in his office. I'll bet half your cousins were conceived on a desk—no offense, Lola. Don't let them get to you. You're right, they should have knocked."

I still feel so ashamed.

"Will Julian be fired?"

Oliver says nothing, holding the phone to his ear. Then: "Yes, right away please. Back to her apartment."

Guess there's my answer. The phone settles back in the cradle with a click, and my heart sinks down to the floor.

"The car will be waiting for you. Want me to take you home?"

I shake my head. I've caused so much trouble already, but maybe Oliver sees how I'm holding on by a thread, because he huffs and grabs his jacket.

"Screw it. I'm not going to listen to them yelling at each other. Bunch of babies."

Julian's not a baby. He stood up for me in there, and now he's going to get fired, and what have I done? Run away like a coward. I hover, staring at the door, until Oliver takes my elbow.

"Come on, Lola. You can't help Julian now. Let's get out of here."

\* \* \*

Maybe I can't help Julian, but I can send a damn text. I write it in the back seat of the car, typing angrily and then deleting it all again, trying to figure out the right thing to say. The words that could help Julian.

When I finally press send, a weight lifts off my shoulders.

*Uncle Ray. I know you're upset by what you saw, but I'm not happy with you either. We shouldn't have done that in the office, you're right, but you shouldn't have yelled and treated me like a child. You said a lot of cruel things, and you were very rude to the man I love. I hope you didn't get Julian fired, because that's the man I'll marry one day. Remember that you're dealing with your future nephew-in-law.*

Maybe it's presumptuous to think Julian will want anything more to do with me, and he's definitely never suggested he'd marry me, but Uncle Ray doesn't know that. He doesn't know we haven't said the L-word, and it's the best protection I can offer Julian right now. I show Oliver and he nods, jaw tight.

"You tried your best, honey."
I'm not so sure.

# Julian

Well, I was supposed to make partner in three months. Instead I'm packing up my office, tossing my belongings into a cardboard box while the sunset scorches the city behind me. Vance and Irving didn't even fire me, the spineless idiots, they just withdrew the promotion. It's clear now that I'll *never* make partner in this firm.

Assholes. As if I'd stay here, whipped and tamed. And as if I haven't caught them doing far worse in their own offices. They're covering their asses, trying to keep Ray Briggs happy.

"What will you do?" Oliver leans against my office wall, watching me pack up. "Apply to other firms?"

I grunt. That's the obvious option, but I don't know if I have it in me to bow and scrape to another set of fools. "Maybe. Or maybe I'll set up my own firm." Lord knows I've got the contacts by now. Most of Irving & Vance's clients request me by name.

Oliver brightens. "Will you take me with you?"

I glance at him, but he's serious. Huh. Well, that's something. "I'll need some time to set up. A few weeks, maybe a month before I can start paying you."

Oliver beams, bouncing over to my desk, and fuck, that enthusiasm is just like Lola. My gut twists. "Okay, I'll wait here for a few weeks. Don't leave me behind, though."

"I won't."

She left *me* behind today, but I know that's a petty thing to think. Who can blame her? Her uncle broke her heart right in front of our eyes, and then we were all too busy yelling and dick-measuring to see her slip out. What was she supposed to do, force a bunch of angry, old-fashioned men to take her seriously after seeing that? They made their minds up about her as soon as they stepped into the office.

Of course, they still take *me* seriously, even her uncle. Hypocrites, the lot of them.

I suspect Oliver had something to do with Lola's escape, but I haven't asked. I don't mind. I'm grateful.

"She sent a text to her uncle," he says suddenly. "Told him to be careful, because he's dealing with his future nephew-in-law."

I snort, heart lifting. She was only trying to protect me, obviously, but for a warm moment I can pretend it's true.

Maybe Lola *could* love me—even after this shit show.

Maybe I could marry her one day.

"Mr Rodriguez?" I grunt, dropping an armful of files in the box. Oliver inches closer. "You'll go and see her, right? I really think she needs you."

Lola needs me? I pause, a stapler in one hand.

I've kept my distance all afternoon. Didn't pester her with calls or rush over to her apartment. I didn't think she'd want to see me at all; didn't think she'd want the reminder. I mean, it's not like she said goodbye or left me a note. She just *disappeared.* Vanished into the air like smoke.

But if she does need me… if she's been waiting for me all these hours…

I drop the stapler with a clatter. "I'll pack up the rest tomorrow."

Oliver grins, herding me back through the door. "Tell her you love her!"

"Stay out of it, Oliver."

"And bring her flowers! Or—no—cake pops!"

I stride down the hallway and jab the elevator button, heart racing. "You watch too much TV. I'm serious. It's not a good look."

Oliver cackles all the way back to his desk. The doors swish apart, and I step into the elevator, swallowing hard.

Enough bad shit for today. I'm going to find my girl.

\* \* \*

Lola doesn't answer the first buzz. I hover on the sidewalk, throat tight, and buzz again, speaking into the grate in case she can hear me. "Lola? It's me. Ah, Julian. Will you let me in, please?"

There's a deathly long pause. My hopes rise and die, one by one, in this pause. Goodbye, hopes.

Then there's a *click* and I shove the door open, heart pounding.

A chance. That's all I need. One chance with her.

I need to make this right.

My shoes smack against the tiles, then I take the stairs three at a time. By the time I reach Lola's floor, there's a stitch in my side and my shirt sticks to my back. I did not think this through. And I can't even recover, because her door opens and then she's watching me. Leaning in the doorway with her arms folded. Dressed in blue silk pajama bottoms and a white camisole.

"Lola," I wheeze. I can't fucking speak, my chest heaving as I catch my breath. "Shit. Sorry. I ran."

Her mouth twitches, but she frowns as I thrust my gift in her direction. I came here via a late night bakery, and they were happy to arrange the cake pops like a bouquet of flowers. Pink and white and lemon yellow cake pops, all round and sweet and covered in sprinkles.

Is this dumb? It feels dumb.

Lola takes the bunch of cake pops from me gingerly, clearing her throat.

"It was Oliver's idea," I say quickly, throwing my assistant under the bus. "He said you needed me."

Lola hums, and she won't meet my eye. I straighten and move closer, finally recovering from my sprint up the stairs, and her chin wobbles when I tip it up so she'll look at me.

"Do you want me here, Lola? Or should I leave? I can't blame you after what happened today, but I've been—I'm—even a few *hours* without you have been torture."

Lola sighs, then takes my wrist and pulls me inside. I follow her lead, though I can't read her at all. Where is my chatty girl? Her slumped shoulders make my stomach churn.

"I'm so sorry, Lola," I tell her once we reach the kitchen. She turns to face me, pale and silent. "They were right. I never should have put you in that position. You are very precious to me, and I let that happen. It's the worst thing I've ever done."

136

It's true. It's all true. I've been kicking myself all afternoon, dragging myself over hot coals. Do I seriously think I deserve this girl after all that?

Lola scoffs. "You're a lawyer, Julian. I doubt that."

My mouth twitches, but she's not smiling yet, so neither can I. "Oliver told me you texted your uncle."

Her head tilts. "Did it work?"

Ah. Well. No, not really, and at my silence, she folds in on herself. "I'm not fired," I say quickly, "but I can't work there anymore either. Not if I want a real career. Please don't worry about it," I add, because her eyes are damp, and *fuck*, I hate seeing Lola cry. "I'm going to start my own firm. Oliver's coming with me."

A watery smile. Thank god. "You sure you want to hire that brat?"

At last. I'll take every scrap of humor from her, every sign that she's okay. "Yeah, I guess so. Even though he told me to bring you those stupid cake pops." I wave at where Lola set them on the counter, and this time when she looks at them, her expression softens.

"Don't be mad, but I'm kind of sick of cake pops right now. And sick of… playing make-believe."

Fuck. Her uncle is the worst. I cross to Lola and take her by the shoulders, then give her a gentle shake. "Don't listen to that for a second. What you built is real, Lola. You sold all those cake pops today, didn't you?"

She nods, chewing her lip. I swoop down and kiss it until she sighs, melting against my chest. Her hands tangle in my shirt. "Maybe I will keep going with Sprinkletown. But without all the help and favors this time. Just me, figuring it out."

I squeeze her, so proud. "You'll be great. And it will mean

more that way."

"Yeah."

For a long while, we stand there in silence. Leaning against each other for support, her soft bits pressing against my hard body.

"That was my first blow job," Lola whispers after a while, and she sounds so sad. So mortified. I rest my chin on her head, holding on tight.

"It was so good, my Lola. Forget the way it ended. We'll rewrite it this second, and say it ended as it should have—with me spilling down your pretty throat. We'll say you sucked the life out of me, and then you licked me clean with your kitten tongue. Then I spread you out on my desk and returned the favor."

She pokes my rib. "Maybe I would have spit. You don't know, Julian."

I tut, shaking my head. "Onto my clean carpet? Lola, we talked about this."

Her laughter is a balm to my tired soul. And when she takes my hand, dragging me to her bedroom, I send up a silent prayer of thanks.

She's okay. *We're* okay.

Everything else is mere details.

\* \* \*

"I haven't done this before." Lola's lying flat on her back, naked and flushed, one palm braced on my abs like I might dive on her and ravish her at any moment. She's not wrong, especially since she took such delicious care in peeling off my clothes. "So you'll have to be gentle."

I lean over her, offended. "I'm always gentle. Was I rough with you just now, when you came all over my chin?" I bend down and wipe my beard on her shoulder, demonstrating exactly how much she liked it, and Lola kicks and squirms, her laughter floating up to the ceiling.

"Stop it! God. You're such a jerk." But she's grinning, pulling me closer.

Now, that won't do. I'm a lawyer to my core. "When you say 'stop', mi amor, do you mean I should climb off?"

Lola huffs. "We're not in court right now, Julian." She hooks one leg around my hip, trying to guide me down, but I resist her.

"Indulge me."

By Lola's long sigh, you'd think I was the most tiresome man on Earth. "Okay, no, you infuriating man, I don't want you to stop. I want you to f–fuck me."

Hearing her stumble over that word makes my cock twitch and my chest ache. I brush stray pink strands of hair off her forehead. "Tonight, Lola? You're sure? We can wait, you know. According to your text, we have the rest of our lives—"

She lunges up with a growl, silencing me with her mouth on mine.

She thinks I'm teasing. And maybe I am a little, but I mean it too. As far as I'm concerned, this is my future wife, and I'll wait as long as she needs.

I think, though, if I delay any longer, Lola will scream at the ceiling, so I reach between us and position my cock at her center.

I go slowly, like she said. Gentle and sweet. Nudging inside her, inch by inch, feeling her tight channel stretch around me. A few times, Lola whimpers, and I pause. Wait for her hips to roll again and for her nails to claw my back before I press deeper.

Fuck. She's scorching hot and so wet. Gripping me, *squeezing* me.

"Lola," I rasp, licking at her throat. Nipping her earlobe. "Fuck. You feel like heaven on Earth. You were built for me, sweet girl. Do you like my cock pushing inside you?"

She moans in answer, her nails digging into my shoulders. Her hips rock up, and I slide deeper. *Deeper.*

Yeah. I like it too.

"Good thing they didn't walk in on *this*," I say, and she scoffs and smacks my side. My laugh vibrates through both of us, and fuck, I've never felt this close. So connected, so intimate. So at home.

When our bodies seal flush, we let out twin groans.

I'm sweaty. She's flushed. My arms shake where they're braced at her shoulders, and I can still taste her pussy on my lips. It's messy and awkward but perfect, too, and once we find our rhythm...

I see stars.

"*Shit*, Lola." My hips slam into hers, pounding her up the bed, and she clings to my damp neck. Arches her back and moans. "Do you have any idea how perfect you feel? Such a good girl. Such a—"

She surges up, flipping me onto my back. I grin, chest heaving, as she scrambles up to straddle me, swinging a thigh over my hips.

She's got me. I'm conquered.

# *Lola*

⁓❧⁓

"Yes, my love. Sit on my cock. Just like that." Julian hisses as I lower down, taking him inside me again, and I grin as I start to move. It takes a second to get my knees in a good position, then we're off, my hips rocking and ass bouncing.

"You're so freaking *chatty.* I did not see that coming. You've got that silent, broody lawyer thing going usually."

I love it, though. There's no room to wonder whether he's having a good time, because Julian sings my filthy praises, loud and clear. And it's a relief, because this feels so freaking good to me too. Like toe-curling, heart-pounding, make-your-hair-stand-on-end good.

The wet noises between our bodies as our flesh slams together... they're obscene. And he's so thick and hard, sliding in and out of my pussy, and the air is heavy with the smell of sex. My inner thighs are pink from Julian's beard rubbing me there, and my clit still tingles from being sucked until I came.

It's wild. I feel like I should be more ashamed, more shy

about this, but I'm not. Even after the disaster in his office, how could I be self-conscious when Julian stares up at me like that? Dark-eyed and hungry? Praising me, so reverent.

"Fuck," he says, licking his bottom lip. "Look at your titties bounce."

See? I snatch his hands off my thighs and put them on my tits instead, and Julian growls in approval. He's all too happy to pinch my nipples until my clit throbs. Then he pushes to sit upright, and the new angle makes my breath seize.

He's *everywhere*. Pressing against my clit from behind; his dark belly hairs tickling it from the front. I scrape my nails over the ridges of his abs, and he chokes out a laugh, tensing. "You're a demon, my love."

I start to roll my hips again, not bouncing up and down, but grinding on him. God, that feels perfect, and pleasure floods my body like a shower of warm sparks.

"You're going to come on my cock, Lola." He sounds so freaking confident. So arrogant, and it should not be sexy, but here we are. I loop my arms around his neck, nodding in a daze, and Julian nips my chin. "You feel that? It's the only cock you'll ever need. You're *mine,* Lola Briggs, and I'm going to fuck you every day until you admit it."

I mean, I already know I'm his, but if that's the threat... I could take a few weeks before I tell Julian.

Because this is the best thing I've ever felt. I'm so alive. So grounded in my body, but flying at the same time.

And it's different from when I came on his tongue. This time it's slower and deeper, rolling over me like thunder, and I can't do anything except cling to Julian's shoulders and hold on for dear life. I buck and whimper. I shake and moan. And his long, satisfied sigh—it almost sends me over the edge a second time.

"*Yes*, Lola." He bucks up into me, quick and hard, then warmth blooms between us, and that feels so good too. "*Fuck*."

I slump in his arms, sweaty and sticky and breathless.

It's so perfect. Then my stomach growls.

Julian chuckles, tracing his fingertips up and down my spine. "Guess you're hungry for a cake pop after all."

\* \* \*

*Four years later*

My husband's office is my favorite delivery. Sprinkletown has dozens of workers these days selling cake pops in skyscrapers through the city, but I always take this building. Maybe I'm the jealous type—but more likely, I need my Julian fix. After all, it's been *hours* since he woke me up with his face between my legs.

I cross the lobby, a large box of cake pops balanced in my arms. I'll start on the lower floors and work my way up.

Julian's firm is in a smaller building than Irving & Vance, but personally, I think it's nicer. The rooms are brighter, with big windows and art deco tiles on the ground floor, then polished floorboards above. *No carpet,* Julian told me once with a smirk. Whatever. There are still some rugs I can aim for.

There are fewer lawyers working here too, but the ones Julian has are the best. Killers, Oliver calls them, draping himself over the copy machine to flirt with the older women.

I don't care if they're vicious. They're all suckers for my cake pops, so that works for me.

When I first brought a delivery here, Julian asked if I wanted him to tell them all I was his girlfriend. I told him no. I'd had enough 'favors' from my Uncle Ray, and I wanted to do things properly this time. Julian just smiled at me. God, it makes me so gooey when he's proud.

And they bought so many cake pops. Julian was right—it felt even better since I did it myself.

Of course, *now* they recognize me. The firm is four years old, and I've been Julian's wife for three. A few jump up when they see me coming toward their desks, but I don't think they feel pressured to buy my cake pops. Mostly, they're worried about my swollen belly.

I save the best for last. The sexy grump himself. Oliver whistles when I walk past his desk, half empty cake pop box held aloft, and he waves a hand at my stomach. "You have a license to drive that thing?"

Yeah, twins look ridiculous on me. "Shut up, Oliver," I tell him sweetly, then pause with the box. "Double chocolate cake pop?"

A minute later, Julian lurches up behind his desk when he sees me too. He rounds it quickly, then crosses to take the box off me and spreads a hand over my stomach. "I wish you'd make Oliver do your dirty work."

"I don't think that's in his contract."

Julian grunts, sliding one hand around to rub circles on my lower back. "One of your own minions, then."

Yeah. I *am* tired. Maybe I'll stop now until the babies are born—especially if it smooths that worried pinch to my husband's forehead. I reach out and smooth it with my thumb. "You fuss too much."

Julian leads me to his chair, expression sour. It creaks like crazy when I sit down, and my sore feet tingle with relief. "I fuss the exact right amount, thank you."

"So *grumpy.*"

Julian smirks, then sinks to his knees in front of the chair. He backs up until he's half hidden under the desk, eyes sparkling with mischief. "Did you lock the door?"

I bite my lip. "No. Did you?"

Julian shakes his head, flipping my skirt up my thighs. "Oh, dear. Will we never learn?"

He's teasing. Oliver knows better than to come in here without knocking, and besides–what's Julian going to do? Fire himself?

"I bet you're an absolute tyrant of a boss."

Julian hums, rubbing his cheek on my thigh, and he doesn't deny it. "Lola, my love, I learned it all from you."

Ha. Well he said it, not me. "Come on, minion," I tease, grabbing a handful of his hair. "Get back to work."

## III

# Filthy Headlines

# Description

**M**y gorgeous new boss doesn't trust me.

**Guess I can't blame him. I'm an undercover reporter.**

Grant Keller isn't just a billionaire. He's a well-known grade A jerk, known for his ruthless business dealings and cold demeanor.

There's no one Grant hates more than the press... but that's too bad. Because he's hiding something, and it's my job to find out what.

One month into my new job as a reporter, my boss sends me undercover. I'll work for Grant, find the secrets of his business—and expose him, once and for all.

But Grant's not what he seems. He's complicated... intense...

even *sweet*, especially with me.

And now I'm falling for my undercover mark.

# Sasha

*ne month earlier*

O The press pool is crammed. I squeeze my way between the narrow rows of chairs, tripping over leather satchels and stepping around abandoned takeout coffee cups. Most of the reporters here are men, and twice my age too. Pushing through in front of me, my editor Simon blends in perfectly: with his soft brown blazer and mane of shoulder-length salt and pepper hair, he's everything I'm not.

Older.

Male.

Successful.

I'm working on that last one.

"Come along, Sarah."

That rich British accent would probably be more fun if he'd remember my name. But after a full month in the newsroom, setting up my desk and trying to prove my worth in my new job, Simon has still only learned the first letter.

"It's Sasha, sir."

I hop awkwardly over another reporter's outstretched legs, shooting him the side-eye. What, he couldn't even *try* to let me through? The man stares back at me, his face somehow bored and aggressive at the same time. And you can see the exact moment he registers that I'm not exactly like all the other reporters here.

I'm young—fresh faced and eager, straight out of college.

And I'm undeniably female, with my blonde hair braided back in a bun.

The man smiles broadly and moves his legs, the gesture coming way too late.

"Thanks," I say flatly, pushing along the row after Simon.

The man's eyes follow me, hot and itchy on my back. And this is everything I feared when I chose a career in journalism. *Male-dominated*—that's the word for it, right? Thinly veiled code for: *You're not welcome.* And: *We're gonna make this hard on you.*

Screw 'em. If these men can't see past a pencil skirt, they've got no business writing the news.

Simon stops at the first two available seats, bending down to brush a scrunched up ball of paper off my chair. He smiles at me too, as we lower into our chairs—a quick tug at the corners of his mouth before he's back to business.

He's not so bad. Not a sexist jerk, anyway, even if he can't remember my name. Which almost makes it harder, because now I care what he thinks. I want to impress him so badly, it keeps me up at night. Simon is exactly the kind of mentor I've dreamed of since college.

Rigorous in his research. An unstoppable reporter. When he gets hold of a story, he never lets go.

I'm going to be like that. And this press conference—this marks my first chance. My first big assignment.

It all comes down to Grant Keller.

We're here a few minutes early, never mind that the room is already crammed as full as a sardine tin, so I take a moment to flip through my notes. Grant Keller's latest launch is his third major project in as many years—each a bigger success than the last. Property, media, tech—you name it. He's done it, and he made it look easy.

Now investors look at him with dollar signs in their eyes; well-dressed women in fancy bars all around the city are sizing him up for a ring. He's the Midas man—everything he touches turns to gold—and yet when he steps into the room, a vicious ripple runs through the press pool.

Reporters freaking hate Grant Keller. And not just reporters, either.

He's prickly. No—he's an asshole.

And there's something suspicious about him. I *know* it.

Simon knows it too. That's why we're both here, instead of a lone junior reporter sent to record the announcement. That's why he keeps darting me quick smiles, paying more attention to me than he's done all week.

My editor pulled me into his office before 8am this morning, and gave me my first assignment. I'm going undercover. Working for Grant Keller.

I lean closer now, my arm brushing against Simon's blazer. The press pool is a sea of scowls and angry mutters as the man we're all here to see strides to the podium.

"Isn't this risky? What if he recognizes me?"

Simon stifles a laugh and shakes his head. He points at the front of the room with his pen, his notebook balanced on his crossed legs.

"You see that man?"

"Yes." Well, duh.

"He's not looking at us, Sarah. Not as people. Grant Keller hates reporters—when he looks out at us, he sees a pack of braying wolves."

I chew on my lip. "And he won't be surprised to find a braying wolf turn up to work as his assistant?"

Simon shrugs and straightens up. "I daresay he won't notice you at all."

Ouch. Okay, that shouldn't sting. The whole point of going undercover is that I can fly under the radar. But even in this crowded room, with way too many hungry eyes on my back, it doesn't feel great to hear your boss call you forgettable.

I clear my throat. "Good. That's good. And it's Sasha, sir."

"What?" Simon frowns at me, confused. Then the murmurs die down, and we turn forward.

Grant Keller stands at the podium, scanning the crowd with open distaste, one hand pushed loosely into his pants pocket. Dressed in a dark tailored suit and crisp white shirt, his collar open at the throat, he looks more like Clark Kent than any of these reporters. Thick dark hair. A square jaw. The swell of sculpted muscle under his suit.

Grant's pale gray eyes are cold enough to freeze us to our seats, and yet everyone else seems used to it. They bristle, they grumble quietly, but no one else seems to hold their breath.

I do. Something about that cold, empty gaze... my heart skitters in my chest, tripping over its own beat. When his eyes pass over me, scanning quickly over my cream blouse and laminated press pass, I duck my chin, staring so hard at the notebook in my lap that the letters blur. And when his gaze roves on, I slump back in my chair.

I feel weak. Flushed. Like I've run five miles, not sat still for ten minutes.

"There," Simon murmurs. "You see? He didn't even blink at you. There's no risk of recognition."

"If I get caught at his office…"

Simon raps his pen against his notebook. "If you are unable to perform this assignment, there are plenty who will."

"No! I can do it." The words tumble out, tinged with panic. "I promise. I'll find whatever Grant Keller is hiding."

The man in question clears his throat, and silence spreads through the room. When he speaks, his voice is deep: a smooth baritone. It doesn't match his frosty glare.

"Keller Enterprises is delighted to announce the launch of our latest initiative—an AI tool the likes of which the world has never seen…"

He doesn't sound delighted. Someone should tell his speechwriter. Grant Keller sounds curt. Like this is all a huge drag.

"No oversight." Simon mutters under his breath as he scribbles notes. Does he know he's doing that? Or is it for my benefit? "Risks to jobs. Not regulated by the law."

I hurry to keep up, dashing off my own notes, turning page after page in my notebook. For a man who clearly hates press conferences, Grant Keller is an excellent speaker. Clear and confident. Not rushing or tripping over his words. But after five pages of notes, I see why all the journalists hate him.

He's not giving us *anything*. Nothing that really matters. Everything he's said, we could get off the official project website—and I already did, before we left The Courier's office this morning.

When he opens the floor to questions, it's no better. Grant Keller dodges every question they ask, only ever giving the sparest crumbs of information. It's almost impressive—he gives just enough that it was worth us coming here, but not enough for a good story. It's all too polished. There's no angle.

Simon gusts out a breath. "I loathe this man," he murmurs as the last questions are wrapped up. "Grant Keller thinks he's above scrutiny."

I watch the man at the podium closely. Is that what's going on? From where I'm sitting, it's more like this conference is a chess game, and Grant Keller is the master. He'll walk out of this room with everything he wants—publicity for his project; a public statement he can refer people to; another *screw you* to the press—and everyone else will leave with scraps.

We'll resent him, sure. We'll try even harder to bring him down; to find the skeletons in the closet that a man like Grant Keller must surely have.

I mean, you don't become a billionaire by thirty five without getting your hands dirty. Grant Keller is hiding something.

But whatever it is, we haven't found it yet. No one has. And whoever breaks that story—their career will be made.

It's going to be me. As I watch the icy cold billionaire step down from the podium, striding from the room without a word of thanks, I feel the certainty in my bones.

None of these reporters have broken him yet.

But I will.

# Grant

"Sir?"

The voice drifting out of the speakerphone on my desk is tentative. Not a good sign. I sigh and sit forward, bracing my elbows on the polished wood of my desk.

"Tell me, Derek."

"There was another power outage. We lost… a significant amount of data."

Perfect. A headache throbs behind my left eye, and I stifle a groan as I rub my temples. It's not Derek's fault, even though he's my project manager. It's no one's fault—except perhaps for mine. In this company, I'm the top of food chain. The final stop. It all comes back to me.

Debilitating power outages aren't something we predicted. They've certainly never been an issue before. But we'll sure as hell have measures in place now.

"You need help putting in a plan?" *Say no*, I urge in my head. I'm a big picture man—all these fiddly little problems, the putting out small fires, is the worst part of these launches.

Businesses can be so goddamn needy.

Besides, what am I paying these people for? In a few months' time, I'll have moved onto my next big idea, and they'll have to deal with this crap without me.

"No, I've—I've got it." I'd feel a lot better if Derek said that like he meant it. He's young for the position I put him in, only a few years out of college, but he's sharp. Hungry.

Now we just need to hone his killer instinct.

"In terms of funding—"

"Use whatever you need." It's not like we're hurting for money. And more to the point, none of my people would dare misuse funds. I have zero tolerance for that shit.

"Okay. Thank you, sir. I'll update you with our progress later today."

"Can't wait," I mutter, once the call has safely ended.

It's always like this. When I start a project, there's the rush of a new idea. Everything is shiny and exciting, brimming with potential, and each day thrums with adrenaline.

Then there's the launch. And sure, that means dealing with those morons in the press, but I get a nice fat payday to make up for it.

But then... there's this. The interminable stretch after launch, when my new idea has lost its shine, but it's not well established enough yet for me to leave it on autopilot. I still have to be here, at my desk or at the end of a phone, ready to babysit at a moment's notice.

Answering stupid questions.

Shepherding this project to the point where it can stand on its own.

And forcing polite smiles—or at least, not cursing everyone out when I can't.

*Nightmare boss.* That's what my last assistant called me in an online review two days ago. *A sadistic son of a bitch.* The press had a field day with that tidbit.

My suit stretches against my shoulders as I push to my feet. All around me, my office is a blur of polished glass and rich bronze. Aged wooden bookcases and leather hardback tomes. It's a mix of modern and classic, technology and antiquity, and even the most insipid reporter could spin a personality piece out of five minutes in here.

They never will, of course. This whole building is off-limits to the press, along with the rest of my life. When I caught some asshole picking through my garbage last week, hoping for a scoop for his paper, I called 911 with a smirk on my face.

They won't get anything out of me. Ever.

The press has caused me enough heartache.

Morning sunshine spills through the shining glass walls, lighting up the plush cream rug on the floorboards. I shrug my suit jacket off with a sigh, draping it over the back of my chair before rolling my shirtsleeves to my elbows.

Might as well get comfortable. I've been here for hours already, and the day has just begun. There will be more panicked phone calls, more desperately boring meetings. More mundanity before I can get out of here and blow off some steam.

I'm pacing back and forth along the glass walls, the city skyline at my shoulder, when a harsh buzz sounds on my desk. I pause, confused for a moment, before I remember: it's the direct line to the desk outside. No other sound is quite so grating, such an attack on the fragile peace in here.

No one has pushed that button for five days.

My new assistant must be here.

\* \* \*

My standards for assistants are simple. I want them to answer my phones. Deal with stupid emails. Stand between me and the constant wave of nonsense coming my way, making sure that only top priority issues get through.

If they can pick up a coffee order and refrain from chatting—even better. And in return, I'll pay them better than any other boss in the city.

My deal breakers? They're simple too.

No small talk.

No personal calls on company time.

And absolutely no digging into my private life.

If this new assistant can follow instructions, use common sense, and mind their own business… we'll get along just fine, newspaper articles about the *nightmare boss* be damned.

My footsteps drum on the floor as I push out into the corridor. My office is on the top floor of the Keller Enterprises skyscraper, and there's only one other desk up here. It's generously sized, standing further down the corridor opposite the elevator bank, and for the last five days, the cushioned desk chair has been empty.

It's not empty now.

My strides falter. I recover quickly, tugging at my shirt collar.

Unlike plenty of businessmen in the city, I do not have a track record of deliberately hiring beautiful assistants. Not only do their appearances have nothing to do with their job performance, it always seemed a foolish distraction. Why the hell would I choose to split my own focus? Amateurs.

My last assistant was in her sixties. A fine woman, I'm

sure—besides her regrettable personality—but old enough to be my mother. And before her, my assistant was a man.

*This* assistant... could be a challenge. I slow my steps, prowling closer to her desk. She hasn't heard me coming yet, the sound of my footsteps muffled by the corridor's rug, and she's bent over behind the desk, rummaging in a bag on the floor. Her golden hair is braided up over her head in some kind of fiddly crown, and it shines where it catches the light.

"Where the hell did I... *shoot.*"

She curses to herself quietly, shaking her bag with a rattle.

"Lost something?" I stifle a smile as she jolts upright, her mouth stretched in a perfect 'o'. She's painted her lips in a muted red, and her dark fitted dress hugs an hourglass figure.

Someone hired a fifties pin up model as my assistant.

Fuck.

"Mr Keller!" She drops her bag to the floor, wincing at the loud thump. But she forges ahead, pushing to her feet and offering a dainty hand. "I'm Sasha Jones. Your, um. Your new assistant."

Her palm is cool and dry. I shake it carefully. "Yes, I assumed as much."

"I'm so glad to be here, sir—"

I talk over her, dropping her hand and stepping back. "Let's skip all that, shall we? You're pleased to be here. You're happy for the opportunity. I'm sure you'll do well—etcetera, etcetera."

"...Right."

Is that a spark of irritation in her eyes? They're surprisingly difficult to read, despite being so big and brown.

No matter. She can hate me as much as she likes—as long as she does her job.

"My last assistant left in something of a hurry."

Her red mouth twitches. "I heard."

So she read those articles. Wonderful. I grit my teeth and round her desk, leaning past her to click at her computer. I bring up everything she'll need, logging her in and checking it all works.

"As a result, there won't be a handover. Everyone has their hands full with the launch, and I'm far too busy to train you, so you'll have to learn as you go." I glance over and find her closer than I expected. Close enough to hear the soft draw of breath through her nose. "Understood?"

She nods once, curt.

Leaning over the desk like this, I catch the faint scent of her perfume. It's subtle. Warm. Like honey—or vanilla. Sunshine made scent.

I straighten quickly, clearing my throat.

"You'll field my calls. Deal with my emails. Manage my calendar and take notes at meetings. Plus carry out any other ad hoc tasks I deem necessary."

Her eyebrow lifts a fraction, but she says nothing. My eyes snag on her pulse, thrumming at the base of her throat.

"Any questions?" The words come out in a rasp. Fuck, this was a terrible hire. I need to get rid of her.

"Yes, actually."

She watches me closely before she speaks, and I get the oddest sensation. Like I'm being stripped to the bone—pulled apart and examined under a microscope.

What a weird assistant.

"What are your priorities, Mr Keller? If I'm going to assist you well, it would help to know your goals. In the business—and beyond."

"My business goals are as you would expect. Profit and

progress. Beyond?" The headache flares back to life in my skull. I pinch the bridge of my nose, annoyed. "*Beyond* the business, my priority is privacy. Never ask about my personal life again, Miss…"

"Sasha," she clips out.

We fall silent, both strained.

I linger for a long moment, and what the hell am I waiting for? Another wry smile from those dark red lips?

Something tells me another smile isn't coming. And it's just as well, because I don't want one. My own teeth are clenched as I round her desk, eating up the corridor with long strides, plunging back toward the peace of my office.

To work here, all Sasha needs to do is mind her own business.

And that question—that's strike one.

# Sasha

Three days later, I step out of the elevator at 8am to a rhythmic pounding floating down the corridor. It's violent, mixed through with pained grunts.

Is Grant Keller... in a fight?

That would make one hell of a story. I drop my bag on my desk and hurry towards his office, my heels sinking into the rug.

"Mr Keller, are you alright?"

His door swings open beneath my palm, and the question dies in my throat.

I've been in here a few times already. Staring around with wide eyes, trying to soak it all in and commit it to memory. And each time, I noticed something new. An artistic sculpture; a high tech gadget. An abstract painting on the wall.

But somehow, I never registered the huge treadmill tucked away in one corner, partly hidden by a screen. It's matte black with sleek lines and sharp corners—the sports car of running equipment.

And sprinting on top of it, elbows pumping and jaw clenched, is Grant Keller.

No: Grant Keller… in a suit.

"Um."

I step further into the office. It's still dark on the street outside, the rows of city windows glowing yellow.

"…Sir?"

His scowl burns into me in the mirror on the far wall. He doesn't even slow down. "What do you want?"

Hmm. What do I want?

I want to know why he's sprinting like wild dogs are chasing him, instead of doing a normal person's workout. I want to know what time he gets here in the mornings. I want to know why he's running in a freaking *suit*. And I kind of want to place my hand between his shoulder blades and feel those muscles flex in his back.

Most of all, though, I want to drag him off that treadmill and push a glass of cold water into his hand. My new 'boss' is wild-eyed, with a light sheen of sweat on his handsome features. His muscles bulge under his suit, so powerful as he runs, but I don't miss the way his hands shake.

What do I want?

I guess right now, I want an answer to my question.

I try again. "Are you alright, sir?"

His scowl deepens. "Is that a personal question, Miss…"

"Jones," I grind out. "Sasha Jones." What an asshole. I've spent the best part of three days in this man's pocket, and he still doesn't know my name?

He must sense my concern dropping away, replaced with cold anger, because he prods a button on the treadmill. The machine slows but doesn't stop, and his sprint turns into a loping walk.

Good. Fine. At least he won't fall on his ass.

"I expect you to knock before you come in here."

"Yes, Mr Keller."

"And there will be no more questions about my well being."

"Noted," I growl.

His mouth twitches in the mirror, like he can sense exactly how much I dislike him. With a deep breath, I smooth my face clear.

Now that he's slowed down, I can look at him without worrying he's about to fall and break his neck. Mr Keller is dressed in a navy suit and pale blue shirt, the collar starched against his throat. He's clean shaven, his body bright with vitality, but his eyes are shadowed.

Interesting.

I shift my weight between my feet, ignoring the flush creeping over my skin. Seeing him being so physical… it does something to me. Makes my stomach flip and my heart race. My traitorous brain can't resist picturing certain things—things like Grant Keller jumping off that treadmill, prowling over here, and crushing me back against the door.

The heat of him.

The smell of his fresh sweat.

Oh god, am I panting?

Pale gray eyes narrow as they watch me closely in the mirror.

"Are you alright, Sasha?"

I lift my chin. Marshal my thoughts. "That sounds like a personal question, Mr Keller."

"I pay you to answer questions."

"No, you pay me to answer phones."

Grant rolls his neck, watching me as he strides along the

treadmill. Nerves skitter up my spine.

I can't get fired. If I lose my job here, I'll lose my real job, too. The one I actually care about.

So I arrange my face into a smile. "Perhaps if you put your question in an email, I'll get to it."

My tone is light, teasing, but he only grunts in reply. Then I scramble out of there like I'm the one being chased by wild dogs.

His office door closes with a snap behind me. I curse Grant Keller under my breath all the way back to my desk, my legs wobbly under my pencil skirt.

It's more than an hour until my cheeks cool.

\* \* \*

"Sasha, I need you."

God, I hate the way my belly tightens when he says that. Grant marches toward me down the corridor, dressed in a fresh dark blue suit and crisp white shirt. His black hair is damp where it curls around his ears—so there's a shower in his office.

Crap.

That's not a mental image I need right now.

I straighten in my desk chair, hitting a key to make my monitor go dark. I'm not an idiot—I'm not writing up my undercover notes *here*. But I don't want Grant Keller to know I've been staring at his most recent email for the last ten minutes.

*From: Keller, Grant*
  *To: Jones, Sasha*

*Subject: Personal query*

*Since you refuse to answer such questions in person, Miss Jones...*

*Are you well?*
  *GK*

The hypocrisy. When I first read that email, I glared at the screen so hard my eyes nearly crossed. It took several minutes for my breathing to stop sounding like a raging bull's, and when I finally calmed down enough to reply...

No. I couldn't do it. I sent him my Out of Office notice instead.

That tiny spark of rebellion doesn't even seem to have registered. Grant sweeps past my desk, a briefcase held in one hand and a bottle of water in the other. He swigs from the bottle as he jabs the elevator button with his other elbow, then watches me from under lowered brows.

I squirm in my seat. The leather creaks.

Grant swallows his water and screws the bottle cap down. "Are you waiting for an embossed invitation? We have a meeting in the city. Let's go."

My limbs are clumsy as I scramble to my feet, shoving my notebook and phone into my bag and knocking a cup of pens over with a clatter. Grant's sigh grates against my ears, and I'm flushed bright red when I finally join him in front of the elevator.

*Ping.* The doors sweep open.

Grant gestures for me to walk ahead.

"There was no meeting on the calendar." Even to my own ears, I sound strained.

"This is off the books. A different project."

I perk up, anger fading.

Interesting.

The Keller Enterprises building is one of the tallest skyscrapers in the city, and dozens of roofs and glass windows zip past outside the narrow glass window. I peer out at the street far below, the cars crawling in perfect lines like ants, and sweat prickles across my top lip.

Grant says nothing as I back up, stumbling until my shoulder blades meet the elevator wall.

Then: "Afraid of heights?"

I take a measured breath. Hold it for three seconds, then let it out slowly. "No personal questions, sir."

He hums, and a smirk flashes across his features. "I find counting backward from ten helpful."

With one eye screwed shut, I rap on the elevator wall behind me. Hard enough to sting my knuckles. That dizzying view... "Gosh, I didn't know you could count."

He stares at me for a long moment, the ground still dropping out beneath us, and the words I just said out loud trickle through my brain. Cold dread follows, icy sweat prickling down my spine, and oh god, I'm going to be fired—

Grant tips his head back and laughs.

And if I thought his speaking voice was nice...

His laugh is decadent. Rich and golden; the sort of laugh you could bottle and sell for thousands. If Grant Keller's laugh was a cologne, I'd dab it on my wrists. I'd spray it on my pillow, bury my face in it, and scream.

"It's the window, I think." He moves to block my view of the street. Not difficult, with shoulders like those. "Heights never used to bother me either before this elevator."

"Why don't you change it?" It's not like he doesn't have the money. Grant Keller could plate over that window with solid gold.

"Seems wasteful." He shrugs. "It's only a short ride."

As if to demonstrate his point, the elevator *dings*. The ground settles beneath us, and the doors sweep open to the marble lobby. We step out, Grant nodding at the Keller Enterprises employees hurrying back and forth in pristine suits.

Safely behind him, I smooth my palms down my skirt, checking my sage green blouse for creases. I'm dressed appropriately for an office—a normal office, that is. But Grant's expensive suits and fancy employees make my palms itch. I feel scruffy, even in my best clothes.

"We'll take a car." He addresses me over his shoulder as I hurry to keep up. "You'll sit in on the meeting and make notes. Silently. There will be absolutely no questions. Understand, Sasha?"

My smile is more of a grimace. "Perfectly, sir."

\* \* \*

I wonder how many people get to see Grant Keller like this. Unstudied and off guard—at least, as much as I've ever seen him—sipping from a takeout coffee cup as he reads through a folder of notes for this meeting. Our car drifts slowly through traffic, the windows tinted and the air con cool. And despite myself, I'm sinking against the plush leather seats, my bones melting into the cushions. More relaxed than I've been in days.

"So who are we meeting?"

"Be quiet, Sasha."

My snort echoes through the car. Grant's mouth quirks up at one corner, but he doesn't look away from his notes. And, emboldened by that tiny smile, I only hesitate for half a second before shuffling closer.

His handwriting is messy: the rushed scrawl of someone whose thoughts run faster than they can write. There are pages and pages of notes, crammed together in his folder, and clipped in one corner is a photo. A head shot of a red-haired businessman, with a name printed underneath in black marker.

"Wow. You really are bad at names."

Grant flips the folder closed with a scowl. That tiny smile is a distant memory as he glares at me, gaze cold and unforgiving as it roves over my cheap clothes, my fishtail braid, my scuffed leather bag.

"What part of 'quiet' don't you understand?"

I sit back, crowding against the car door to get away from him. "Sorry, sir."

He stares at me for another long moment, then shakes his head. He turns forward, pinching the bridge of his nose.

And I've learned *some* things over the last few days. For starters, I know a Grant Keller headache when I see one.

"Here." My bag rattles ominously as I tug it open. Honestly, I don't think I've cleaned it out since I bought it two years ago. There could be anything in here. Broken umbrellas; tins of breath mints. Hairbrushes and fliers. Wooden chests of lost pirate gold.

So I'm weirdly proud when I successfully fish a box of painkillers from the depths of my bag. I push it into Grant's hand, avoiding his eyes, and I don't breathe again until I hear the crinkle of plastic. He pops two pills into his palm, then throws them back and swallows them dry.

"Okay, sir." I take back the packet. "No need to show off."

"Sasha." He says my name like a sigh.

I gnaw on my bottom lip for the rest of the drive, fighting the urge to shuffle close again and read over the billionaire's shoulder. The tension is gone, yes, but I don't want to push my luck. And honestly, I'm not sure I trust myself to sit close to him.

Not when his thighs fill his suit pants so well, sculpted from hard muscle. Not when a crazy part of me wants to reach over, bat that folder out of his hands, and perch on his knee in its place.

I'm not here to nurture a crush. I'm not even here to be his assistant. I'm here to unearth this man's secrets—no matter that his deep voice raises goosebumps on my arms.

I fan my cheeks, grateful for the air con.

It's going to be a long day.

# Grant

On my new assistant's first day, I sent an email to HR. *Subject: Regrettable hire.* It was bad enough that I'm attracted to her, never mind that I must be a decade older. That she's so beautiful, looking at her soft golden hair and her ruby lips feels like a heart attack.

No, her real crime was far worse: she asks so many goddamn questions.

The HR manager replied within an hour with a list of suitable alternatives. Other candidates that she'd interviewed, along with a selection of the resumes we keep on file. And I intended to read through them for a replacement—I *did*.

But as the hours and days passed, somehow I never got around to it. And now, two weeks after Sasha began work here, the plan to fire her is a distant memory.

She's... useful. An excellent worker. Quick to anticipate my needs, and creative in her solutions to business problems.

Sasha is almost alarmingly tuned in, her eyes sharp as she looks around the office. That bug-under-the-microscope feeling when she looks at me has never really gone, not when she turns those big brown eyes on me and stares straight into my soul.

Which she does several times a day. Like right now, sipping from the take out coffee I just placed on top of her desk.

"Mm." Her pink tongue darts out, licking foam off her top lip. I grit my teeth, blood surging south. "You do realize I'm supposed to bring *you* the coffee, Mr Keller?"

I manage a casual shrug. "Call me Grant. And I was in the cafe anyway."

*Lie.* I figured out it's her favorite place yesterday, when a half-stamped loyalty card spilled out of her terrible bag onto my rug. And this morning, when I was alone in the office in the predawn darkness, I found myself googling directions. It's only two blocks away.

"I'm just saying. I'm the sunny, helpful assistant who brings you coffee and answers your phone. You're the bad tempered billionaire who forgets my name and goes running in his suits."

Heat crawls up the back of my neck. Fuck, I can't believe she saw that.

"Would we describe you as sunny? I'd say 'shrewish' is more accurate. And that was a one-off."

Sasha quirks a perfect eyebrow. "If you say so. Sir."

The one downside to my blanket ban on personal questions is that I rarely get a chance to explain myself. Sasha will walk in on me in some kind of uncompromising position—stripped to the waist in my office, or running in that fucking suit, or throwing darts at the board on my wall with a vicious snarl—and she'll press her lips together and say nothing.

She probably thinks I'm insane.

If the press spoke to her, I'd be screwed.

"We're staying late tonight. There are four big meetings next week to prepare for." I pause for any sign of resistance. Sasha taps her pearly pink nails on the desk and gives me a sugary smile.

"How exciting."

"Indeed."

"Off the books again?" Her question is light. Almost bored. Something prickles down my spine. Against my better judgment, I ignore it. "Two of them, yes."

Sasha nods slowly, sipping from her coffee. I don't know what the hell I was thinking, bringing her that, but when she hums again in appreciation, I know I'll do it again. Probably multiple times a day if it means she'll make that sound.

"I can't believe you know my order."

I frown. "Why not?"

She levels me a look. "Because most days, you don't even know my name."

That heat prickles over my neck again, and I clear my throat. I need to get out of here. I've got—got work to do, damn it. A launch to oversee. Budgets and deadlines and stress.

"Sasha Jones." I clip the words out. Like I'm mad.

She leans back in her chair, and the first real smile I've coaxed from her all morning curls her red lips.

"Very good, Mr Keller."

"Grant."

"Who?"

I'm storming down the corridor, my office door slamming shut behind me and blocking out her soft laughter. It still echoes in my head, swirling round and round in my brain, and I scrub a hand over my face as I sit behind my desk.

She's a distraction. I really should fire her.

But when another suggested replacement lands in my inbox from HR two hours later, I delete it without looking. Whoever they are, Sasha is better.

* * *

When I insisted we work late together, I didn't account for how intimate it would feel. We're always up here alone, the only two people on this floor, interrupted only by the occasional visitor and the chirp of phones. And we both work long hours, coming in before most others in the building and staying until the streets are dark outside.

But this is different. My shirt is unbuttoned at the collar; my sleeves rolled. And twenty minutes ago, Sasha kicked off her heels with a groan. She's barefoot on my rug.

*Barefoot.*

Her toes are painted the same pearly pink as her fingers. That knowledge will haunt me, I know it.

"Don't start." She holds up a palm when she catches me staring. "*You* try walking in heels all day. It's torture."

"It's fine." My throat is tight. "I'm not going to complain. I'd like you to be comfortable."

Understatement of the fucking century.

We migrate naturally to the floor, the agreement between us unspoken. And now, with my eyes snagging on her bare legs, crossed at the ankle, I'm questioning how smart of a man I really think I am.

The city lights glow through the glass office walls, the pinpricks of stars winking high overhead. The rumble of traffic is faint so far below, and it's like we're the only two people in the world. Marooned in a pocket out of time.

176

Sasha flicks through one of the folders I prepared. She doesn't comment on the photograph pinned to the front paper, but her eyes linger on it.

"You know, I thought the billionaire lifestyle would be more glamorous. Less work, more play. Fewer meetings and more super yachts."

I huff a laugh. "Old habits die hard." I watch her for a moment longer before turning to my own notes. And my voice is casual when I tell her, "I hope you didn't have to cancel any plans tonight."

"Is that right?"

"Of course." There's a long silence. Fuck, she's going to make me ask it. "Did you? Have to cancel plans?"

Sasha flips a page, then pins me with those big eyes. Her plush mouth is twisted in a wry smile. "What exactly are you asking me, Mr Keller?"

*Did you have plans with friends? God, did you have a* date?

*Did you choose me, Sasha Jones?*

"A personal question. Never mind."

Because it wouldn't be choosing me, even if she did cancel plans. I'm her boss—I told her she'd be working late and she agreed without complaint. She's a good worker. Not someone I should ever think of like this.

Sasha sighs and pushes to her feet, her bare toes sinking into the rug. She stands for a second, stretching her arms high overhead, and the taut line of her body is burned into my retinas.

She's wearing a wine red pinafore dress, a cream silk t-shirt underneath, and her hair is tied back in an elaborate bun. The sight makes my fingers twitch and my pulse race—I want to plunge my hands into that golden updo and shake it loose.

But Sasha strolls away across my office, peering openly at my shelves and the artwork on my walls. I watch her go, my notes forgotten in my hand.

"You're very nosy for an assistant."

"So I am."

"Did it bother your last boss?"

She hums absently. "Simon? No. I expect he liked that about me."

Jealousy roars through my chest, blinding and irrational. It's not enough that I hate the thought of her dating—now I'm sick with envy over her last boss too? I jerk my head to the side, glaring down at my notes until the words form into shapes I can read.

A soft inhalation makes me look up.

Sasha stands behind my desk, brown eyes wide. She stares at my computer monitor, and far too late I remember what she'll find there.

A head shot of her, stolen from her HR file. Pinned to the edge of my computer screen, and scrawled on in black marker with her name.

"Grant…"

"Don't ask me." The words scrape against my throat. "Don't ask me about it. I've learned your name, haven't I?"

"You have." She watches me carefully. Like I'm a wild animal she might spook with sudden movements. The dim light from my desk lamp casts shadows across her beautiful face. "But—"

"*Don't.*" I'm breathing hard. Way too hard for someone sitting still, and fuck, this is why I have a treadmill in my office. Why sometimes I have to jump on there without changing clothes. Except Sasha's here, and she'd see, and she'll know something is badly wrong, and there's a high-pitched sound bouncing around my skull—

"Grant." Sasha's kneeling in front of me, her gentle voice cutting through the ringing in my ears. She shakes my shoulders gently. "You're alright. Everything is okay."

I swallow hard. My throat is so goddamn tight, and her hands are so light on my shoulders. Her warmth bleeds through my shirt.

"I'll finish up here." My thoughts are sluggish, but once they're in order, my chest eases. There is a simple solution. "You can go home, Sasha."

"I really don't mind—"

"*Go.*" She flinches back—and yeah, okay, that was way too gruff. I push to my feet, and then we're both standing, the empty air between us impossible to breach. "Thank you for your help tonight."

It's no use. My words are too little, too late, and her pretty face has shuttered. Frost practically crackles over her skin as she bends to scoop up her bag.

"Take tomorrow morning off."

She shoulders her bag. "Yes, sir."

*Grant,* she'd called me. My chest is a ragged hole. She glances at the folders scattered over the rug, but I wave her away.

"I'll deal with it."

"Right." She stomps her feet into her heels, wobbling with her hands spread in the air. I jolt forward, ready to catch her elbow, but she's already wheeled around, marching across the office.

The door slams shut behind her.

Steady footsteps echo down the corridor.

I stand frozen, head pounding.

What a mess.

\* \* \*

It takes fifteen shameful minutes for me to realize what I've done. I've kept my young, female assistant late alone in the office, then sent her out into the dark streets without consideration for her safety. My hands shake as I click angrily at my computer, searching the staff database, and my stomach roils as I press the phone to my ear.

*Idiot.*

She'd be right to hate me for this. I wouldn't even blame her.

*Pick up. Please. Pick up.*

After an eternity of her phone ringing in my ear, the line picks up, and I hear the rumble of traffic. The faint *clack clack clack* of her heels on the sidewalk.

"Sasha. Thank god."

She exhales sharply. "Yes, Mr Keller?"

"Where do you live?"

The address field is blank on her staff file.

"So many personal questions tonight, Mr Keller."

"It's Grant." *Please don't take it back.* "And I'm concerned for your safety. Are you walking home alone?"

Her shoes drum against the sidewalk, answering my question. But she's softer when she speaks again.

"I don't live far. Only a few more blocks."

"You didn't answer either of my questions."

"No, I didn't. Annoying, isn't it?"

"Sasha."

"Grant."

I grind my teeth so hard, I'm surprised I don't crack a molar. It's not like I don't deserve it.

"I shouldn't have sent you out alone in the dark. I apologize."

180

Her snort crackles in my ear. "I'm a big girl. I can get myself home."

"It's not your behavior I'm worried about." I dig the heel of my palm into my eye. "Will you stay on the line?"

Her pause is deafening.

"Please," I grit out.

"There's really no need…"

"Humor me."

I glance around my office as I wait for her answer. She was only in here for a few hours tonight, but already it's colder with her gone. Lonely in a way it's never been. Shadows slope over the walls and warp the artwork; the light from the monitor washes my desk ghostly blue.

I stare at that damn head shot of her, my heart thumping in my chest.

"Alright." She sighs. "God, you're a demanding boss."

"So I've heard." The smile that breaks over my face feels alien. Unpracticed. "But I'll make it worth your while. Ask me anything you like."

On the other end of the line, her footsteps falter against the sidewalk. Then she's striding forward again, marching fast, and I'm sick with hoping I haven't judged this wrong.

I'm not lying. Whatever she asks, I'll answer.

I only hope I won't regret this conversation.

There are hundreds of questions I've dodged from her over the last two weeks. I fully expect her to repeat one of those, or god help me, to ask about the head shot pinned to my monitor.

But instead, Sasha clicks her tongue, then asks: "If you could have any superpower, what would it be?"

It's such an innocent question. So sweet. And it's like a show of faith—I've given her a free body shot, and she's refused to

181

take it. Asked something harmless instead.

Warmth spreads through my veins like liquid gold.

"Invisibility." My answer comes easily. "No doubt about it."

"Really? Why?"

"No press." She says nothing, so I shrug and keep going. Staring at her photo while I talk. "No people trolling online. No one watching my every move, waiting for me to fail, hoping and praying that I'll slip up and do something unforgivable. I could work, and create, and be left alone."

"Is that what you want?" Her voice is small. "To be alone?"

"No." And somehow, she manages to get a confession out of me anyway. Because I'm still staring at her photo. "Not totally alone."

I've said way too much. Maybe not spelled it out for her, but surely she must hear the longing bleeding into my tone? I grip the phone so tight it creaks, and when she tells me quietly that she's arrived home safe, it's equal parts pain and relief.

"Good. That's good. Set your security alarm when you go in."

"I don't have an alarm."

I pinch the bridge of my nose. "You—"

"Goodnight, Grant."

The line drops with a soft click. I stand there for a long time, breathing hard and trying to untangle the sharp feelings balled up in my chest.

Then I place the phone back down. Trace a fingertip along the edge of her head shot.

And stride out of my office without looking back.

# Sasha

⸎

Grant Keller is... not the monster everyone thinks. The knowledge is a queasy thing, sitting low and heavy in my stomach, as I spend more and more time with the reclusive billionaire.

First, there's the security alarm—installed in my apartment one day while I'm at work.

Then there's the box of designer sneakers left on my desk one morning with a note. It's Grant's messy scrawl—as if it could be from anyone else around here—and it says: *For your walk home.*

I sit for almost an hour, staring at those sneakers. Fiddling with the laces, my chest squeezing tight. And when I try them on after a full day of heels... it's like walking on a cloud.

But it's the elevator incident that really kills me. We're bundled in the glass and chrome space together one afternoon, riding up to the top floor after another meeting in the city. And we're chatting about nothing, flicking through our pages of notes, when the electric light overhead flickers before winking out.

The elevator hushes, slowing to a halt, and all around us is the *tick tick tick* of cooling metal and the ragged sound of my breaths.

"It's alright."

Grant looks paler than usual, but his voice is steady. Calm. He guides me back away from the window, until my shoulder blades hit the opposite wall and his fingers wrap around my bare forearm. His touch is warm and dry, sending nerves sparking under my skin, and my breath leaves me in a *whoosh*.

"Hello? Yes. The thirty-eighth floor." He talks to maintenance with the same calm voice, and all the while his thumb sweeps back and forth over my wrist. Back and forth.

"Grant." Even my whisper sounds strangled. He crowds closer, his shoulders blocking out the window completely as he keeps talking into the metal grate, and his heat washes over my front.

"Keep us updated, please. Yes. Thank you."

As soon as he's done talking to maintenance, Grant turns the full force of his attention on me. His chin dips, his pale gray eyes raking over my trembling lip, my ashen skin, my heaving chest.

"Wow." His voice is light, teasing, but there's an undercurrent of strain. "You really do hate heights."

"I do *now*."

His laugh rumbles through the small space as I yank him closer, burying my face in his chest. And okay—it's easier to forget we're in a tiny metal coffin hundreds of feet in the air when his cedar and spice cologne tickles my nose. When his arms wrap around me, crushing me tighter against the hard planes of his chest; when his pounding heart thumps beside my cheek.

"If I'd known this would be your response, I'd have sabotaged the elevator myself weeks ago." Grant's fingers play with stray tendrils of my hair, and what the hell am I supposed to do with that?

I know what I *want* to do.

I want to push up onto my toes and bury my hands in his dark hair.

I want to trace a circle around his voice box with my tongue.

I want to feel the hard length of him—the one currently pressed against my stomach—against other, more sensitive parts of me.

But I can't do any of that, so I settle for muttering, "Liar." He's teasing, anyway. He'd never trick someone into this.

Because Grant Keller isn't the asshole everyone thinks he is.

So it's a relief in more ways than one when, six minutes later, the elevator hums back to life. We untangle ourselves slowly, stepping away with forced smiles, and when the doors slide open, we race to our separate desks without looking back.

Of course, those sneakers are waiting for me, lined up neatly on the rug. So I collapse into my desk chair, bury my face in my hands, and groan.

What the hell am I doing here?

* * *

It would be bad enough if Grant were my boss. My *real* boss, with my career in the palm of his hand. But the reality is somehow even worse—because it's not Grant who starts calling me every day, his clipped, impatient tones in my ear.

It's Simon.

"What do you have for me, Sasha?"

At least he's learned my name. I guess that happens when you're a big disappointment.

"Nothing. I—nothing, sir." I bite my lip, leaning over my desk to check Grant's office door is closed. It's a risk for Simon to call me here. His patience must be coming to an end. "Mr Keller is bored of this project. He's putting out feelers for his next enterprise."

But none of that is *news*. It's a clear pattern for Grant—one the press has already analyzed in a hundred op-eds.

Simon's sigh rattles down the handset.

"*I could have told you that, Sasha. What on earth have you been doing there for the last two months?*"

Writing fluff pieces about the city's business scene. Spinning articles out of the people I meet with Grant; the conversations I overhear.

Nothing that will impress my boss.

I squirm in my chair. There is one thing I could mention—one thing I've never read about Grant in the papers. His panicked sprints on the treadmill in his office, and those head shots in his folders, with names scrawled in black marker.

It means something. I know it does.

But those things are too personal, somehow. Handing them over to Simon—it feels like the worst kind of betrayal. So I swallow hard, and drum my nails on the desk.

"I'll find something, sir. I promise."

"See that you do."

*Something* walks through the elevator doors two hours later, and my stomach sinks. This is it. My in.

The woman has short, brown hair curled up in a bouffant, and a chunky necklace rattles against her chest as she strolls to my desk. I recognize Tina Belsham from an old security pass in my desk drawer—she's Grant's last assistant. The one who wrote that scathing review.

She has the face of a person who would do that. Like she's been dipped in vinegar.

"Hello." My face feels rubbery as I force a smile. "May I help you?"

In the end, it's way too easy to make polite conversation. To hand over the paperwork she's come to collect, and slip her Simon's business card at the same time. Tina Belsham's eyes light up, her penciled eyebrows twitching up her forehead, and she looks at me again with fresh interest.

She knows. She knows I'm a reporter. That I'm here undercover, lying to Grant.

I want to crawl under the desk and curl up in a ball.

Afterward, as the elevator hums back down to the ground floor and I'm left sitting alone at my desk, my stomach rolls so much I think I might throw up. This is my job. It's the whole reason I'm here.

So why do I feel like crying?

\* \* \*

The article comes out two days later. I know the exact moment Grant sees it: he curses loudly, the sound echoing down the corridor, and then comes the telltale *thump thump thump* of his treadmill.

I time him—he stays on there for nearly an hour, pounding away with angry strides. And I bring up Simon's article on my computer, one eyed screwed shut as I read.

It's... not so bad. It's balanced, at least—Simon is a good

reporter, not some tabloid idiot. He relays the woman's complaints, but he's quick to show her bitterness too. I'm relieved to see he's unearthed the reason she was fired and included it in his write-up, and if anything, Grant comes off quite well. As firm but fair—not a bad boss at all.

It could have been so much worse.

My legs shake as I push to my feet.

His office is quiet when I nudge the door open. The sound of his shower floats through the closed door to the en suite, and papers are strewn across his desk. The article glows on his computer screen, and I wander over. Close the tab.

The photo of me is still pinned to his monitor.

"You saw it? The article?" Grant steps out of his en suite a minute later. He's dressed in a clean black suit and sage green shirt. His jaw is hard as he tugs his sleeves straight.

"Yes. Grant... it's not that bad. They actually paint you in a favorable light—"

His head twitches to the side, like he's shaking off my words. And when he strides over to the desk, his steps are jerky with anger.

"The goddamn Courier... the press are vultures, Sasha." I turn to leave, but he catches my wrist. His eyes burn into me, his face so close. There is barely any space between us. "Don't worry about working here, alright? I'll protect you from them. I'll never let this shit happen to you, I promise."

The room tilts to one side as I nod.

Grant's thumb sweeps over my cheekbone. This close, I can smell his shampoo. The soap from his shower. His hand cups the side of my face, and god, I've spent so many hours staring at his hands.

They're big. Strong. With long fingers and squared knuckles, and intriguing calluses on his palms. I've laid in my bed so many nights already, imagining how those calluses would feel dragging along my bare stomach; I've imagined him grabbing fistfuls of my blouse and tearing the buttons open.

"Grant."

I sound choked. Way more worked up than he is, with his shadowed eyes and smooth face.

"Is this okay?"

His murmur vibrates down to my bone marrow. My chin jerks in a nod.

He exhales hard, spreads one palm over my hip, ducks his head, and seals his mouth to mine.

The kiss stops the breath in my lungs. It lights up every nerve ending in my body; it sends heat surging through my limbs like wildfire. I sway up on my toes, gripping Grant's shirt with both hands, and moan into his mouth, my hips pushing against his.

I want him. I want his taste and his heat; I want the crackle of anger still simmering under his forced calm. I want to wring the same desperate noises from him that he coaxes from me, and more than anything, I want his strong body driving into mine.

"Fuck. Sasha." Grant plunges his hands into my hair, pulling my bun loose. Waves cascade down my back, and his groan curls my toes—but that's nothing to the desperate *want* that surges through me when he takes a handful of that hair and tugs my head back.

I blink up at him, lips parted.

He scowls down at me, pale eyes molten.

Our breaths are ragged, mixing in the air between us. Then, as quickly as it started, it's over. Grant drops his hold on me, stepping back, and his face shutters before he turns to look out of the window.

"I shouldn't have done that. It was inappropriate." He glances at me, sprawled over his desk with flushed cheeks, and his voice drops lower. "Forgive me, Sasha."

My nod is clumsy. But trying to gather my limbs, trying to make my body work again—that's the real disaster. Picking my way back across his office in my heels, I'm more like a baby deer learning to walk than a real human being.

"It won't happen again." Grant's quiet promise behind me burns in my chest. I don't turn back to look at him. I can't.

His door closes with a snap.

# Grant

I shouldn't have kissed her. If the press knew I did that…
Well. It doesn't matter what they'd write. I still
shouldn't have done it.

It's easy to tell myself that when I'm alone in my office, or
during the rare hours I spend in my penthouse apartment.
With a safe distance between us, I can be rational. I can remind
myself that Sasha is an employee, and far too young for me
anyway. That she's nosy, and infuriating, and she pushes my
buttons more often than she calls the elevator.

With that space between us, I can't believe how foolish I've
been.

But the moment she's near to me again, all my good sense
evaporates into a fine mist. Suddenly, my heart thumps against
my rib cage like it's counting down until I kiss her again. My
ears strain to hear her every soft breath, every rustle of her
clothes, and I breathe the scent of her perfume in like I'm
trying to imprint it on my lungs.

I still bring Sasha those ridiculous coffees. Wait like a

starving man for her answering smile.

And when I lock myself in my en suite, a full length of corridor and two doors barricaded between us, I jerk my cock like I'm punishing myself. With every ounce of the self loathing boiling in my veins.

I come like a freight train, hissing between my teeth. And when my pulse slows, I want to slam my head against the wall.

There's a simple solution, of course. To keep my distance. It's not like I kept Tina fucking Belsham in my pocket, and that was only partly because she was so useless. It's not *necessary.* I built my first business all alone, and that's still my preferred mode of operation. An assistant is a formality, nothing more.

But I've grown used to having Sasha with me. Murmuring her sharp insights after business meetings, leaning close so her breath tickles my throat. Sensing my black moods when they descend, and lifting them with her teasing jokes. Handing over those goddamn painkillers when my skull begins to throb, like it's a sixth sense.

So I don't think twice before inviting her to a formal business dinner in the city.

She'll be useful.

That's all.

* * *

Sasha is not useful.

She's a fucking goddess.

The most beautiful woman I've ever seen, dressed in a bottle green cocktail dress, her golden hair woven into some kind of intricate braid.

She always wears it like that. Fiddly and pretty and neat,

those stray tendrils mocking me with how badly I want to wind one around my knuckle.

"Is this okay?" She smooths nervous palms down her hips, and I want to howl at the night sky. I'm such a fool.

"Yes. You look—yes. Come on."

I pretend not to see her flicker of disappointment, because what else can I say? I sure as hell can't tell her how fucking badly I want her, how one glimpse of her in that dress makes me want to toss her over my shoulder, go straight back upstairs to my office, spread her out on my desk, and *feast.*

Her heels click against the marble lobby floor. I check my stride, walking slower.

"Where is this thing?"

"In the Emporium. A half hour drive away."

And wow, I did not think this night through. If I'd been paying attention, if I had an ounce of sense, I would not have asked her to climb into a darkened car with me. Not ever, and certainly not dressed like that.

"Sorry." Our knees brush as we settle against the leather seats. I slide further away, and try not to see the flash of hurt in her eyes.

The car coasts through the evening traffic, painfully slow. Sasha keeps up a brave attempt at conversation, flicking through the folders of notes I brought in preparation.

Each one has a photograph clipped to the first page. She still hasn't asked me about it.

"So what's the goal tonight? Scoping out your next project?"

"Something like that."

Her mouth twists, but for once I'm not dodging her. I've barely thought tonight through. Since she started working for me, I've been distracted as hell. Coasting on autopilot, all my usual business fervor redirected.

Aimed at her.

Even though I'm being poor company, Sasha rallies like a champion. She makes polite, charming conversation over dinner with the elite business figures at our table, displaying a level of knowledge that makes something tickle at the back of my brain.

She's no usual assistant. She's a major player in her own right, steering the conversation effortlessly and digging up pearl after pearl of information.

The longer the night wears on, the heavier my chest weighs.

But it's nothing. It's nothing. She's intelligent and curious, that's all.

By the time dessert is over, I'm ready to leave. My head's not in this, and I'm not getting anything useful here—better to retreat home, and get safely away from that bottle green dress. But something makes me pause as we stride across the Emporium ballroom together: the quiver of strings drifting through the air.

"Oh," Sasha says softly.

*Oh* is right. The lights have dimmed, the ballroom lit with low-hanging lamps that look like stars, and all around us, couples sweep onto the dance floor. Normally, I wouldn't even break stride, but Sasha's eyes are so wide. Filled with yearning.

The words escape before I can stop them. "Dance with me."

She stares at my offered palm like it's a grenade.

"Grant…"

I shift my weight, determined now, and don't drop my hand. What, would it be so terrible? I won't step on her damn feet. I'm an asshole, not a klutz.

Sasha leans close. Her perfume wafts over me as she whispers.

"The press will be here. People will see."

And suddenly, for the first time since I was fifteen years old, I don't give a shit about the press. They can write what they like—take whatever photos they can steal of me.

Her fingers are cool in mine.

"Sasha. Listen to me. I don't care."

And maybe that was bravado, but when she steps into my arms, it becomes truth. She's so graceful, bowing elegantly against me as we turn, and as she smiles up at me, she bites her red lower lip. We spin slowly, weaving between the other couples, and the soft, aching string music echoes down to my soul.

"I like this," she murmurs. "I've never slow danced before."

Fuck. I want to be all of her firsts.

Holding her like this—it's agonizingly familiar. It brings those other times rushing back—cradling her against my chest in the broken elevator; feeling her melt into me when I kissed her by my desk. And it brings back all the times I've dreamed of kissing her, too: a heady whirlwind of images that has swirled around my brain for months.

Every morning chat over the coffees I bring her. Every short ride in the elevator together. Every time she's stepped into my office, knocking softly on the door, her neck craning to make sure she can come in.

Sasha peering up at me, lips parted.

Her chest heaving beneath her thin blouse.

Her pulse tapping frantically in her throat—just begging for the scrape of my teeth.

"Sasha," I grind out, and I don't even know what I'm asking.

Only that if she says no, something will fracture inside me.

Her hand tightens around mine. She leans close, lips brushing my earlobe.

"Let's get out of here, Mr Keller."

\* \* \*

The car is hushed. Dark. Warmer than the frosty night outside, but still cool enough that goosebumps ripple over Sasha's bare arms. I reach over, scowling at the partition between us and the driver, and take her wrist. Guide her across the leather seat and into my lap.

"Wow. Um." Her thighs settle on either side of my hips, her fingertips sliding around my neck to play in the ends of my hair. "This is new. I've thought about this before, actually."

"Tell me." It's an order, curt and low, and she shivers. Shuffles a fraction closer, her dress brushing my shirt.

"Well. Okay. It's not so much one time in particular as every—every time we were in here together."

*Fuck.* "Go on."

My palms stroke up and down her thighs as she talks, soothing her nerves and hitching her dress higher. Bare skin meets my thumbs, feverish now, and I draw tiny circles. Relishing her softness.

"Well, mostly—mostly you were being an asshole. Usually. But sometimes, when you smiled at me or held the door or I caught a whiff of your cologne, I just wanted to reach over and knock those stupid folders out of your hands and… and…"

She trails off, her blush radioactive even in the darkness.

"Sasha." I grip her thighs and squeeze. "I won't ask you again. Tell me."

Her breath shudders through the car. Raindrops streak across the tinted windows, glittering as we pass beneath streetlamps, and there's only the purr of the engine and the steady *thump* of my heart.

Her nails scrape against the back of my neck. She chews her lip.

"Sasha."

"Okay. Okay. It's just—" She frowns at the base of my throat "—you have nice thighs. Sort of... strong-looking. So I wanted to sit on your lap, and feel you being all sturdy beneath me, or slide off the seat and kneel between them and—"

Her chin ducks. Like she's considering doing it now. God, I've had the exact same thought, along with a hundred other things I'd like to do to her, in the back of this car and in every other location. But though her words have heated my blood like nothing else, have made me hard as stone in my pants, the first time I touch her will not be like that.

It won't be about me.

After all these weeks together... I want to make her sigh.

"Good." Slowly, I hitch her dress higher up her thighs. She's warm and smooth and trembling. Practically panting already. "Good girl."

Her scoff is half-hearted. And she chokes it back, swaying with hazy eyes when my thumbs skirt the edges of her panties.

"I'm going to touch you now."

"O-okay."

The fabric is damp. Burning hot.

"I'm going to make you come."

A shaky inhale. "Yes."

"Would you like that?"

For the first time since the ballroom, she meets my eyes.

197

Sasha scowls at me, irritation mingling with glassy-eyed arousal.

"Grant. Don't be an ass."

"You have to say the words. Come on, Sasha Jones." My thumbs slide the barest fraction beneath her panties. "Ask me to make you moan. Beg me for it."

"Shit." Her forehead drops to my shoulder, and now her hips are working. Rocking her core against my fingers. "You're so cocky. I should not be into that."

"But you are." I hook her panties to the side. When my fingers meet her heat, she lets out a broken moan.

"But I am."

I capture her mouth in a kiss. I can't hold back anymore, not when her breath is hitching and she's so hot and slick, rolling her hips against me with abandon. Each little moan and sigh that escapes her lips, I swallow it down, greedy for every noise she makes. And when I slide a finger inside her, rubbing against the vice grip of her pussy, I thrust my tongue past her lips and fuck her mouth too.

"G-Grant..."

A growl rumbles in my chest. She tastes so fucking good. Like champagne and honey and *Sasha*.

I've done this a thousand times in my head. And I knew, I fucking *knew*, that she'd be like nothing and no one else. That she would wreck me.

But knowing it and experiencing it are two different things, and I could never have imagined the way my heart would pound when she moans, nearly slamming clean out of my chest. I never pictured my throat growing tight, clogged with longing, and I didn't realize that her fingernails would dig almost all the way through my jacket as she clings to me, clutching my shoulders.

I'm blind-sided.

There's a smoking crater where I used to be.

"Grant, I think I'm going to—"

"Do it." I thrum her clit, so turned on my teeth ache. "Give it to me, sweetheart. Show me how pretty you are when you come."

It happens like a thunderstorm. Slowly at first, then building, building, until she's locked in a maelstrom in my lap and I can't tear my eyes away from her. Her mouth drops open; her thighs shake. The *sounds* she makes.

I'll never recover.

When the car pulls up outside her apartment a minute later, I'm startled. I thought we'd have longer. But Sasha glances out of the window, chuckles softly, then brushes her lips against mine before sliding off my lap. I'm gratified to see the tremble in her legs.

"I'll see you in the office, Mr Keller. Thanks for the dance."

The door slams shut, and I watch her shadow race across the rain-drenched sidewalk.

# Sasha

"I want to come back in."

Simon sits opposite me in my favorite cafe, stirring an English breakfast tea with his mouth pressed in a firm line. Raindrops sprinkle his mane of dark hair, and his brown blazer sags over the back of his chair.

All around us, shoppers sip at coffees, bags clustered around their table legs, and executives page through newspapers with bored expressions.

"Now, Sasha? When you've just begun to make progress?"

I kick at my chair legs. "You said yourself in your article. Grant Keller is a good boss. Well, he's a good man. There's no dirt to find."

Outside the cafe windows, rain blows down the street. It's early evening, and yet it's as dark as midnight already, the raindrops flashing in the glow of the streetlamps.

I take a deep breath. Firm my shoulders. And press my palms into the table.

"The Courier is a serious newspaper. Correct?"

Simon huffs. "Obviously."

"And you sent me to Keller Enterprises because we thought there was something seriously wrong. Something unethical, something *illegal*. But I'm telling you—I've been there for two months now. Grant is private, yes, and he has his quirks, but there is nothing worthy of proper news." I bite my lip, then go for the jugular. "Anything we find will be tabloid gossip."

Simon straightens. He places his teaspoon down with a *clack*.

"We're not interested in gossip." He says it like a dirty word.

"I know."

Simon is a good man, too.

My boss watches me intently, drumming his fingers on the table. Steam curls over the rim of his mug, and I wrap my hands around my own coffee, anchoring myself with the heat.

This whole conversation is a risk. I'm a brand new reporter, fresh out of college. There are literally thousands of new graduates like me, people who would kill to take my job. Who would dig into Grant Keller's secrets without even a flash of guilt.

I distract myself from that thought with a sip of my drink, humming at the hot, sweet coffee as it spreads over my tongue.

"Sasha."

Simon seems... awkward. It's a strange look for him. Normally, he's every bit the head editor of a major newspaper—confident and canny, all power and poise. Half the junior staff are in love with him, and the other half are too afraid to look him in the eye.

But right now, Simon's fiddling with his spoon like it's suddenly the most fascinating thing he's ever seen. He clears his throat and pushes the spoon away, spearing me with his gaze.

"Are you certain you are… objective about Grant Keller?"

"I… I'm sorry?"

A muscle tics in Simon's temple. But he keeps talking, his voice sure and low, all clipped British vowels. "He's an attractive man, by all accounts. Intelligent, successful, charming—"

I snort so loud a man three tables away looks up from his paper. "Grant Keller is not charming. Believe me."

Not in the way Simon means, anyway. He's not *seductive*; he doesn't have slick manners or easy charm. Grant Keller is aloof.

Until he snaps in the darkened back seat of a car, anyway. Then he's all grasping hands and heated kisses—so freaking intense that my breath catches just thinking about it.

Simon sips his tea, eyebrows drawn together, and I shift in my chair.

There's a pulse drumming between my legs. Should not have thought about the car.

"Look." I knit my fingers together. "I like Grant. I won't deny it. He's… compelling. When you get to know him. But—" I lean forward, holding Simon's gaze "—even if I hated him, there still wouldn't be a story here."

"Hm." Simon's chair creaks as he sits back. The spots of rain on his dark blue shirt are drying, and he seems to measure his next words before saying them out loud. "You know, there is rather a pattern in this city of powerful men seducing their employees. Taking advantage of their power."

I swallow, suddenly queasy. Grant's nothing like that. "Not just in this city, I expect."

Simon's mouth quirks. "No, indeed. But that sort of

behavior... that is a headline."

He pauses. Lets his unasked question hang there between us, his face smoothed into a mask of patience. This is how he must coax his stories from his sources: by making it clear that continents could shift and empires could rise and fall, and Simon would still be sitting there, waiting for an answer.

My fingers shake as I reach for my mug. His eyes drop to them, but he says nothing.

When I find my voice, it comes out in a croak. "Grant Keller isn't like that."

"No?"

I shake my head. I don't trust myself to say anything else. I won't—I *can't*—lie to my boss—but I won't incriminate Grant in this, either.

There were two of us in the back of that car. I wanted everything he gave me and more.

"As I said, sir." I raise my chin; pretend my cheeks aren't bright red. "There's no story at Keller Enterprises. And I'd like to come back in."

Simon sighs, clearly disappointed, and my stomach sinks. I've worked so hard for this job. I've dreamed about becoming a journalist. And this assignment was a special opportunity, a chance to prove myself.

"One more week." Simon's tone brooks no argument. This is not a negotiation. "One more week of real investigation, and if you are still sure there's no story, you can come back in. Leave Keller Enterprises behind. But Sasha?"

I nod, fighting the triumphant smile spreading over my face.

"You're a reporter. Don't forget why you're there. Once he realizes who you are... Grant Keller certainly won't."

\* \* \*

Simon's words echo in my head all the way down the sidewalk. It's cold out, the coldest night of the year so far, and the wind and rain blow straight through my coat and chill me to the bone.

*Don't forget why you're there... Grant Keller certainly won't.*

Who am I kidding, daydreaming about the billionaire? I've been ridiculous since the dinner last night—practically floating up to the ceiling every time I think of him. Ever since Grant touched me in the darkness, my nerves have been sparking under my skin. Every sense is heightened; every small thing makes me smile. I dreamed of him all through the night, tossing and restless in my bed, and couldn't help beaming every time he walked past my desk today, his gray eyes hungry when they raked over me, crinkling into a smile.

But Simon's reminder brings me crashing back down to earth.

Once Grant knows I'm a reporter, he'll never forgive me.

My fingers are numb as I pull out my phone. This is the worst kind of masochism, but if I only have one more week with him... I want to hear his voice.

"Yes?"

The blunt answer makes me blink. For a sickly moment, I think I'm busted already, and I won't get that week at all. But then Grant sighs, the sound rattling down the phone, and keeps talking.

"What do you want, Sasha? I'm a busy man."

Okay.

Not busted, then.

Just pining over a jerk.

"Nothing," I rasp when I finally find my voice. "I just wanted to talk to you. But it's not important. I'll see you tomorrow—"

"Wait." Another sigh. Grant could fill a whole symphony with his different sighs, and they always seem to be directed at me. "Don't go. Sorry. I'm just… in a bad mood."

My heels scrape against the sidewalk. I chew on the inside of my cheek, skirting around a glassy puddle. "Why?"

"It doesn't matter." His tone is so sharp, I wince.

"Alright. Suit yourself."

"Where are you right now?"

"Walking home."

"Alone?"

His pointed question makes me blink. "Yes."

There's another pause, and I frown at the cars rumbling past along the street. They're dark, their paint glinting under the streetlamps, and raindrops swirl through their headlights.

"Grant?"

"Sorry, yeah." He sounds lighter suddenly. Happier. "You know, you can take my car home. Any time you like. Just take it."

"I am perfectly capable of walking home."

"Humor me."

I screw one eye shut and force the words out. "Only if you're in there with me."

My heart thumps so hard, I can hear it above the wind. But when Grant's voice drops lower, velvet and intimate in my ear, I know I'm not alone in this. Thank god.

"I've been thinking about that."

"Me too."

"I'd like to do it again. Really commit it to memory."

I huff a laugh, even as heat spreads over my cheeks. "When's your next business dinner?"

"Never, hopefully. But there's a gala on Thursday I can't avoid. Go with me?"

I pull out my keys as I round the corner onto my street, hurrying towards the front steps of my building. "I only have that one cocktail dress."

His chuckle makes my toes curl in my shoes. "Excellent. That dress and I have unfinished business."

There are so many moments when I should really hang up the call. When I reach my front stoop; when I close the door to my apartment behind me; when I wander into the kitchen and open the refrigerator, stomach growling.

But I find myself juggling the phone from hand to hand as I let myself in, squeezing it between my cheek and shoulder as I climb the stairs; then finally putting Grant on speaker and placing it on the kitchen counter top.

He must know I'm home. Must hear that the street sounds have been replaced by a boiling coffee maker and a microwave. But he makes no move to hang up, and neither do I.

It's nice, chatting to him here. Like he's in my home too, warming the quiet, empty rooms with his rich baritone, and that image makes my chest pinch.

"Where do you live?" I ask at one point, fishing a fork out of a drawer. "What's your place like? Wait, let me guess. A big fancy townhouse. No—a penthouse apartment with bare brick walls and a balcony looking out over the city."

Grant sounds pained. "I hate that you guessed that right."

I punch the air, leftover pasta twined around my fork. "Knew it. You're not half as mysterious as you think you are."

"What about you? A shabby chic studio with a hot plate and string lights on the walls?"

I blink around my tiny living space. "I hate you."

"Uh-huh."

"Grant…" The fork hovers over my bowl. My stomach is too snarled up to eat, and I need to know. "Why do you hate the press so much?"

*This* sigh is new. One I haven't heard before. It sounds dredged from the bottom of his soul. But he answers me, the tiredness clear in each word.

"A petty grudge, I suppose. When I was fifteen, my parents got divorced—they were prominent figures, you know? A businessman and an actress. So the press splashed it over the papers for months, made it all so much harder than it already was, and my mother…"

I wait, heart in my throat, until he speaks again.

"She became ill from the stress. And she's never really recovered."

"I'm so sorry." My whisper is too quiet, and I repeat it louder for the phone. "That's—that's awful, Grant."

It is, too. But it's not the type of reporter *I* want to be—it's not who anyone at The Courier is. But I can't say those things now. Maybe I'll never get a chance.

I push my bowl of leftovers away, stomach tight.

"I, um. I'd better go. It's getting late."

"So it is."

"Goodnight, Grant."

"Sleep well, Sasha Jones. Think of me."

*No fear,* I think as I tap my screen, ending the call. Grant Keller has haunted my dreams since my first week in this job.

And I know, deep in my soul, that he'll still be in my dreams long after I've left.

# Grant

I stop the treadmill as soon as the elevator *ping* floats down the corridor. For once, I'm dressed to run in gray sweatpants and a black t-shirt, but I sniff myself carefully before striding out of my office.

She's on time. She always is. I know Sasha's movements now better than I know my own.

8am: step out of the elevator.

8:30: knock on my office door, with a coffee in one hand and her planner in the other, ready to go over the meetings for the day.

Normally, by 8:30, I'm sitting at my desk, studiously not watching the door and clicking through emails. But today, I can't wait the thirty minutes for her to come find me. I set off down the corridor, pulse tapping in my throat.

"Sweatpants, huh?" She smiles at me, sly. Her hair is half-down today, and my fingers itch to run through it. "Must be a special occasion. I thought you wore suits for everything."

"I do." I don't stop at her desk, prowling around the side of it. "To sleep. To shower. You name it."

She looks smaller than usual down there, when I'm standing over her. That pert little nose is level with my waistband, and a primal part of me wants to cup the back of her head and grind her face against where I'm already stiffening.

"There it is," she breathes as I take the arms of her desk chair and spin her to face me. Her plump lips tug up at the corner. "A suit addiction. The *real* Grant Keller scandal."

"Take it to your grave."

She draws a solemn cross over her chest, the swell of her breasts so plump and inviting through her thin blouse. And fuck, why was I such an ass to her last night? When she called me, I practically bit her head off. It's been bothering me ever since, a snide voice whispering in my head that I've screwed it up, and she'll never want to call me on a whim again.

"I'm sorry for being a dick."

She chokes out a laugh. "Can you narrow that down?"

"I'm sorry for being short when you called last night."

Her forehead creases. She did notice, then. "What was wrong?"

Here goes nothing. Better to get it out there; clear the air. Let her know where I stand.

"I saw you. On your date."

She jerks back, startled, and I straighten up, raising my palms.

"I wasn't following you. Nothing creepy, I promise. But you've got me hooked on these stupid coffees, and I walked over there after work, and saw you sitting there with him. The, uh. The old guy. You two looked pretty cozy."

Her nose wrinkles. "Simon's not old."

Fuck. That's the part she's denying? Jealousy flares in my

chest, hot and hungry, and I tamp it down with effort. But when I speak, my words are sharper. I'm only human.

"He's too old for *you*, that's for fucking sure."

"He's forty. You're thirty five."

"What do I have to do with it?"

She gives me a look. "Grant. Give me a break."

And this has gone off the rails. It's not like we're in a relationship—we hooked up once, for god's sake, and everything about this situation is complicated. Just because I'd rather stab a letter opener in my eye than look at another woman now, that doesn't mean Sasha's unhinged too.

I sit back against her desk, crossing my arms over my chest, and search for the right words.

"I don't want you to see other people."

An eyebrow twitch. "Is that an order, Mr Keller?"

Fuck.

"No." I pinch the bridge of my nose. "It's a request."

She must sense the knot in my chest somehow, because Sasha takes pity. A small palm settles on my thigh—tentative at first, then smoothing over the muscle. Back and forth, back and forth, until I melt an inch into the desk.

Every time she touches me, my nerves spark in reply. My heart thumps louder, calling out to her.

"I'm not. Seeing anyone else, I mean. It wasn't a date."

"No?"

"No."

"So Simon is...?"

She frowns at her lap. "A friend. I hope."

"Damn." I tug her to her feet. She hasn't changed out of the sneakers I bought her yet this morning, and without her heels, the top of her head is level with my chin. "I can't begrudge you that."

"Nope. I guess not." Her breath catches as I take her waist, lifting her easily to sit on the desk. Reaching around her, I push her keyboard and planner to the sides, clearing the space, then nudge her shoulder.

"Lay back, sweetheart."

Her eyes are wide as she lowers down to her elbows. I step between her knees, spreading them wider stretching her skirt taut between her thighs. "What are you doing?"

"Typing up an email. What do you think? I'm going to show this pussy why you never need to look at another man again."

I swat her ass, grinding closer to her heat, and she gasps and squirms in response. Her chest heaves, her nipples pointed through her thin blouse, and her fingers hook in my waistband. Holding me in place.

But there's an edge of fear to her expression that I don't like. I pause, the hem of her flippy black skirt pinched between my fingers.

"Shall I stop?"

Her head jerks side to side, her golden hair splayed over the polished wood. "No. God. Definitely not. But, um. The elevator…"

"Mm." I smirk, my knuckles brushing her thighs. "Better keep an eye on it."

*Come on,* I will her privately. *Trust me. Let me taste you.* It's not like I'd ever let anything bad happen to her. And my heart is pounding out a drumbeat as I settle in her chair, rolling close and waiting for her green light.

Sasha purses her lips. She rolls her eyes and tilts her head; fixes her gaze on the metal doors. Then reaches out with one hand, grabs a fistful of my t-shirt and tugs me down to her lap.

*Yes.*

That's the only word that echoes in my head when I'm touching Sasha. When I'm pushing her skirt over her hips, burying my face against her underwear and breathing deep. When I'm slinging her legs over my shoulders, hooking her panties to the side, and finally tasting her heat.

*Yes.*

*Fuck yes.*

She's slick and ready. More turned on than she let slip. And I wonder how often that happens, how many times we've talked or brushed past each other and she's been secretly wet and wanting. I growl against her pussy, the thought driving me higher.

If I get my way, she'll never be left aching again.

"You like that, sweetheart?" My words vibrate against her clit. "You like me spreading you out on the desk, eating your pussy where anyone might walk in and see?"

"Oh—oh god."

I'll take that as a yes.

Her thighs are soft and warm, brushing against my cheeks, and her fingertips scratch against my scalp as she writhes. I lean back a few inches, sliding a finger deep inside her— her moan guts me down to my core.

"Grant. Oh. *Grant.*" Her hips lift as I work her, rolling against the empty air. Sasha's eyes are screwed shut, the elevator long forgotten, and a deep flush darkens her cheeks. "You feel…"

"Good?" I'm ragged. Wrecked.

"So good."

Thank god for that.

I'm so lost in her, focused on her every twitch and moan, that

I don't notice her fingers roving through my hair until it's too late. She finds the scar—raised and jagged, wrapping around my head—and freezes. I still too, breathing hard between her thighs.

"What... what happened here?"

"Car accident," I grit out. "A few years ago." *Don't ask me,* I will her. *Not now.*

Not when she's so close, finally spread out before me on this desk, and I'm living out my fantasies of the last few weeks. Not when her taste is on my tongue and her scent is in my lungs.

Not now.

She parts her lips, like she's going to ask me more questions, so I duck my head and suck on her clit. Slide a second finger inside her and *pulse.*

Sasha bucks and moans, thighs locking around my neck, and when she comes, she trembles enough to bring down the building.

Her breaths fill the room. She lays sprawled on the desk, a beautiful wreck, and I rest my fevered forehead against her knee. I'm so hard, my ears are ringing.

When the elevator light flicks on, we both jump. Then scramble upright, breathless and laughing, tugging her clothes back into place and settling her in the chair.

"Thank you." I hesitate, then drop a kiss on her head. "I'd better, uh—"

"Change your clothes?" She smiles, flicking my t-shirt. "I've got this. Go conceal your weapon, Mr Keller."

I glance down, mouth twisting. Ah.

Her soft laughter follows me down the corridor.

\* \* \*

It's too good to be true. I know that, even with the fact that I'm her boss. Even with the age difference.

I've never been this happy.

Too good to be true.

The feeling builds through the week with every stolen kiss in my office; every time our fingers brush in the elevator. A sense of dread, snaking through my gut and strangling my insides. And I push it away, because Sasha Jones is the best thing I've ever seen.

A golden-haired miracle.

When she meets me in the lobby before the gala, the sight of her is a punch to the chest. It shouldn't be—I saw that dress last week—and yet it's like the first glimpse all over again.

"Ready to charm a bunch of businessmen?" She nudges my elbow as we cross the marble floor.

"Oh, it's not just boring businessmen tonight." I pull the door open, frosty air wafting over our faces. "It's all the power players. Brace yourself."

She's quiet as she settles into the car. I place the usual stack of folders between us on the seat, and we page through them, squinting to read my messy writing. Each one has a photograph clipped to the front page, and I watch her from the corner of my eye. The glow from the passing streetlamps washes over her face and away.

She still doesn't ask me.

"It was a head injury." The words blurt out of me before I even realize I'm saying them. Offering up my biggest weakness on a platter. "From that car accident. I'm mostly fine, but I get a lot of headaches. And I have trouble remembering some things. Like names."

Sasha lowers the folder she's reading into her lap. And her voice is thick when she speaks, addressing her knees.

"I would never have asked you, Grant."

"Well, don't tell anyone." I'm joking, but it sounds too serious in the dark car. I nudge her, aiming for lightness. "If the press got hold of it, my business could sink. No one wants to invest in an entrepreneur with a brain injury."

"But it doesn't affect you. Not in your work."

I shrug. "No, it doesn't."

I wait for what feels like ten years. And when Sasha finally breathes again, it shudders in and out of her lungs like she's fighting tears.

"Hey." I reach for her, tangling our fingers together on her knee. "I'm fine. It doesn't matter."

"Of course it matters," she says, but then she's sliding off the seat and crawling between my knees. Running her palms up my thighs. "*You* matter."

She's tentative as she pulls my belt through the buckle. Lowers my zip, the scratchy sound so loud in the hushed car.

"Sasha," I groan, burying my hands in her hair. "Fuck—your braid thingy—"

"Wreck it." She wraps her fingers around my cock. "I want you to pull my hair."

Holy shit.

Despite her bold words, she's cautious as she brings her red lips to my cock, pressing a shy kiss to the head. Her big brown eyes flick up to me, her grip light, and a new suspicion snakes through my brain.

"Sasha." Her name grates out of my chest. "Have you done this before?"

A tiny shake of her head. Barely visible in the darkened car.

I pinch the bridge of my nose, skull pounding. "And the other things we've done?"

She whispers, "No."

And hell, if I'd known that, I'd have done it all so differently. She deserves silk sheets and champagne, not urgent hands and nipping teeth in the back of my car. She deserves bubble baths and massages and being draped over my bed, not—not being spread out on the desk in front of the damn elevator.

"Sasha." I'm hollow. Hollow, and so fucking turned on.

*Her first.*

Am I really going to do this?

She answers that for me. By squeezing my cock gently, then bring the head to her lips. She drags it around like she's drawing on lipstick, her pink tongue flicking over the slit, and now I can't look away. Can't move; can't breathe.

"Do you want to stop, Grant?" It's a teasing murmur. Her eyes sparkle in the streetlights.

"No." I've got a one-way ticket to hell, but there it is. "Sasha. Suck me, sweetheart. Show me who owns this cock."

She likes that. It's clear from the way her grip tightens, the way she moans low in her throat as she sucks me down. Sasha's head bobs, the stray locks of her hair tickling my thighs, and every point of my focus is narrowed on her.

Her tongue.

Her heat.

*Her.*

She's unsure but eager, and that's so much hotter. Watching her learn me, watching her explore, figuring out what she likes—I'm spellbound.

I grind my hips back against the seat, resisting to urge to

fuck into her pretty throat like it's the biggest test of my life.

"Grant." Her whisper tickles my bare skin.

"Yeah?"

"You're holding back."

True. But—but she doesn't know what she's asking.

"It's better like this, sweetheart. You'll enjoy it more."

"Who says?" She flicks my thigh. "I'll be the judge of that, Grant Keller."

Well, damn. I shift forward on the seat, heat slamming in my chest, and I force myself to find the words—a final note of warning.

"It can be uncomfortable. Some people don't like it. If you want me to stop—"

"I'll tell you. I will."

My breath scrapes in and out of my lungs. "Promise me."

"*Grant.*"

My hips thrust forward, plunging my cock deeper into her mouth. Red lips stretch around me—those fucking red lips. They'll haunt my dreams.

Sasha inhales sharply, her eyes wide at the intrusion, but her cheeks hollow as she sucks, and she bobs her head, urging me on. Deeper. Faster. I cradle her head, her braid a wild mess. Cars drift past on the street outside, and rain patters on the car roof, and I fuck her pretty red mouth.

A few times, she coughs. Splutters when I go too deep. But that seems to wind her tighter, too, until her eyes are hazy and she's swaying in my grip, warm and pliant, and I'm thrusting out a rhythm.

"You like this cock?"

A hum of agreement. The vibration tickles at the base of my spine.

"It's yours. All yours. And when we go into the gala, I'll be stained red with your lipstick."

Another hungry moan.

"Are you wet, sweetheart?"

I know she is. But the reminder gets me what I want: her hand snaking between her kneeling legs. And then we're climbing higher together, our movements getting sloppier, wilder, and when I feel her tensing, coming between my legs, I can't hold off anymore.

"Sasha." Her name tears out of my throat. "I'm going to come. Unless you want to—"

She takes me deeper. Fuck, I love this girl. And I come so hard my brain whites out, her name on my lips like an oath.

Afterward, I fix her up as best I can. Rub her smeared lipstick off her chin; finger comb her hair into loose waves down her back.

"It looks good like this."

She huffs a laugh, shaking it out. I wasn't joking, but as long as she's happy, I don't care.

And Sasha's not just happy, she's glowing, so beautiful I can't take my eyes off her, and when we pull up at the gala, half of me wants to order the car turned around. To take her to my apartment instead, and beg her to quit. To offer her other, better jobs where I'm not her boss anymore, then finish what we started here.

But she's climbing out of the car, the night sky inky black, and I missed my chance.

I step out onto the sidewalk.

# Sasha

The gala is beautiful. A sea of elegantly dressed people, laughing and chatting in the marble lobby of the city art museum. Waiters in tuxedos weave between the guests, champagne trays held aloft, and string music drifts through the perfumed night air.

It's perfect. The kind of event I always dreamed of attending. And my stomach is snarled in knots.

"Stay close." Grant leans down to murmur in my ear, his lips brushing my cheek. I sway toward him, unbidden. "Don't want some famous actor stealing you away."

I snort, but it comes out strangled. "Hardly."

It's laughable—the idea that the gorgeous billionaire would get jealous over *me*. I mean, my dress is creased from the car, and I'm starstruck by half the people here. If the guests notice me, it'll probably be because they think I'm on the wait staff.

But Grant peers at me, so intent, so serious, and I know he means it. I brush my knuckles against his hip, there-and-gone.

"I won't wander. Girl scout's honor."

As if I could. Tomorrow, my last week with Grant is up, Simon's deadline looming over me like a guillotine. I begged him to let me come back, to end this undercover charade, I *know* that, but now that the day's almost here, my heart is raw and bleeding.

Grant will hate me. There aren't many things I'm sure of, but I do know that.

He'll never forgive me.

But at least there won't be any more secrets between us. I've been sick with guilt for weeks now. I can't stand lying to him for another day.

"You stay close too."

I don't know what makes me say it—it's hardly something an assistant can demand of her boss. But the thought of wasting a single second of my last evening with Grant makes my chest tight.

"Don't worry." He's amused, leading me through the crowd with a wry smile. "I'll protect you, Sasha Jones."

Curious eyes follow us as we plunge deeper into the gala. The crowd is thicker in here, interrupted only by pale stone sculptures, perched on bronze plinths. Huge oil paintings line the walls, and a glass chandelier sparkles overhead.

"It's beautiful here."

Grant nods, hand reaching back for my wrist.

"Do you like art? I can't believe I don't know that about you."

My laugh is shaky. He's my boss, not the other way around. Why on earth would he know that?

"Yeah, of course I like art. You know. A normal amount."

His laugh booms towards the ceiling, drawing more pairs of eyes.

"*A normal amount,*" he mutters.

Someone floats a tray of champagne in my direction, and I snag a flute. I'm probably supposed to be professional here, stone cold sober, but what's the point? I probably shouldn't have sucked Grant's cock in the car either.

The memory flushes me hot, from head to toe. I fan my cheeks, trailing after the billionaire's broad shoulders and sipping from the sweet, bubbly champagne.

I'm glad it happened.

I only hope he still feels the same.

*"This is Viola Mackenzie—curator of the gallery."*

*"Bill Yardley—chief of police."*

*"This is Felix Hutchins. An investor of mine."*

Grant introduces me to every person he talks to, and each time they peer down at me, bemused to make conversation with an assistant. I smile and force my mouth to say all the right things, but all I can think of is the stack of folders on the back seat of the car.

He studied for this—to remember people's names. To hide his secret from the press.

From me.

As the evening wears on, the knot in my stomach winds tighter and tighter, and I sip more thirstily at my champagne until my head spins. Grant does all the talking, thank god, and lets me hover nearby, ears ringing, glass squeezed in my hand.

So I spot him first.

Simon.

My boss—my *real* boss—weaves through the crowd nearby. Shaking hands and leaning in to murmur in people's ears. I've never seen him in action before, as editor of The Courier at a major event, but right now, I can see how he charms out these people's secrets.

He's at ease—powerful and slick. At home with these elites; ready to play their elaborate games.

And with his blazer and his wild mane of dark hair, a recorder held loosely at his side, Simon couldn't look more like a reporter if he tried.

"I need—um. Let's get some air." I tug on Grant's elbow, interrupting him mid-sentence. He frowns down at me, concern pinching his forehead, as the stately woman he was just talking to stares down her nose.

"Sasha? Are you alright?"

"Yep. Yes." I pull on his sleeve. "But let's go. Right now." My pulse thunders in my ears. He can't see Simon. Not now. Not yet.

Not when I've got a few more hours left with Grant.

Not when I haven't confessed.

"Has something happened?" Grant stays rooted to the spot, damn him, peering around us. "Did someone say something to you? Something rude?"

And god, even now, he's trying to protect me. I don't deserve this man, and it hurts.

"Please, Grant." I swallow hard and hold his gaze. "I'm begging you. Let's go."

"Alright." He holds up his palms in surrender. His gray eyes are so, so worried. "But you *will* tell me what's wrong outside."

"I promise."

And I mean it. I've always known I'd have to tell him. To look him in the eye and confess my lies.

It will break me. Cleave me in two. But *I* will be the one to tell him. It's only right.

"Come on, then." He plucks the empty flute from my hand, placing it on a passing tray. We're going. We're nearly safe.

But then Grant's turning, his hand taking mine, just as the crowd parts in front of us. And Simon is there, dark eyebrows twitching up as he takes in our tangled fingers; my flushed cheeks; Grant's deepening scowl.

The marble floor drops out beneath me as Grant stills, another stone statue in the middle of the crowd. People flow around us, chatting and laughing, oblivious.

And for the longest moment, I kid myself it's all okay. That he's stopped because of something else—because those folders with their photographs let me pretend.

Those *folders.*

But then Grant drops my hand, and I know. I can't pretend anymore. Cold settles into my bones.

"Ironic, really." Grant barely turns his head to speak, his low voice cutting through the noise of the crowd. Like he can't even bear to look at me. And his voice is bleak, shaking with bottled up rage. "The one time I remember a face. I wonder why?"

He strides off without another word, and that's worse somehow. I wanted him to yell at me. To rant and rave and humiliate me; to hurt me the same way I hurt him.

Instead, I'm left alone and stranded in a sea of cocktail dresses and dark suits. Gasping for breath, the chandelier blurry overhead. Simon pauses, mouth twisting, then steps closer. Nudges through well-dressed shoulders to reach me.

"Sasha."

For once, the editor is lost for words. He frowns at the nearest oil painting, turning the recorder absentmindedly in his palm. Then, with a breath, he pins me with that stern gaze.

"I think you'd better go home."

\* \* \*

Grant won't answer his phone. Of course he won't. I hurry down the museum steps, my phone pressed to my ear, and scan the sidewalk with blurry eyes. Guests spill out of the gala, wrapped in formal coats and silk scarves, and more casually dressed pedestrians weave between them, rolling their eyes.

Next to the curb, a sleek black car idles.

He left me his car. Even now, he makes sure I get home safe. Oh god. What have I done?

"Come on, come on." I rap on the driver's window, waving before I slide into the back seat. "Pick up. Please pick up."

I hold the phone away from my face just long enough to direct the driver back to the office to pick up my things. And when I press it back to my ear, Grant's voicemail message playing over again, I let out a tiny sob.

He won't speak to me.

I'll never get a chance to explain.

What could I say, anyway? Grant Keller has always hated the press, and I'm one of the few who knows it's for a good reason. Because he trusted me, confided in me, and my knuckles turn white where I grip the car door.

It takes forever to reach the office. Even late in the evening, the roads are packed, the rain-soaked vehicles bumper to bumper. So I have plenty of time to replay what happened in my head, hearing his furious words bouncing around in my head.

The leather creaks beneath my thighs. I can't believe we were here together only a few hours ago, his hands in my hair and his taste on my tongue.

I stop trying to call after the twentieth time it goes to

voicemail. His voice is clipped in my ear, telling me to leave a message, and steeling myself... I do.

"Grant. It's me." I clear my throat, voice thick. I will *not* cry to his voicemail. I will not sink that low. "Um. It's Sasha."

I pause, an invisible clock ticking in my head. I was so desperate to talk to him, to explain everything, but now that I'm trying to do it, I'm coming up blank. I'm just sad and tired and sick with regret.

"I'm sorry." Those words are so small. So insignificant. And my words are hoarse as I keep whispering to the empty car. "So sorry. I'm—I'm a junior reporter. I was assigned to work for you undercover. We were—we thought there was something bad going on at your company. Something big."

My eyelids drift closed as a headache throbs behind my right eye. I pinch the bridge of my nose, just like Grant always does.

"I never planned..." Oh god, the things he must think. I swallow, throat tight. "It was real. With us. I need you to know that. I wasn't trapping you. I meant it all."

The car slows, pedestrians passing the tinted windows, and I slink down in the leather seats. It's so cold in here in nothing but my dress, my coat forgotten in the cloak room at the gala. So dark and quiet.

"Look. I..." I don't know what else to say. There are a thousand things to tell him, and nothing at all. "I was going to resign tomorrow. I was going to tell you everything. I know you won't believe me—"

I break off. This is pointless. He'll be insulted to even hear these things. I've told him I'm sorry; told him I truly cared. Anything more is a waste of breath.

"I wish we'd met any other way."

I duck my head, tears streaming.

"Goodbye."

# Grant

I don't listen to her voicemail for three days. And good thing, too, because when I finally hear her say my name, her voice taut with sorrow—

I shatter.

One grueling run, one ice cold shower, and one fist through my office wall later, I make it through the whole message. It's bullshit, obviously. More lies, nothing but lies, and I hang up with a bitter taste in my mouth.

I swig from my takeout coffee, bruised knuckles throbbing, but even the coffee is ruined for me now. It makes me think of her, and seeing her in that cafe with *him*.

The reporter. A friend, she'd said. And as it turns out, her boss. I thought his name was familiar, and now I know why.

I wasn't paranoid—I was perceptive. Better than I'd given my injured brain credit for.

Too fucking good to be true.

Fine—so I listened to her message. I caved to temptation, to my addict's need to hear her voice one more time.

227

Now I can move on.

Of course, I can't actually forget about her. Not when this woman who lied to me holds the future of my company in the palm of her hand. So many of the small things I told her could wreck my future—the truth of my injury most of all. I'm at Sasha Jones' mercy, and it sets my teeth on edge.

"Come on," I find myself muttering every morning in the office, clicking through the business headlines. My heart is a festering lump in my chest. "Do it. Publish it all. Get it over with."

*Put me out of my misery.*

Down the hall, my new assistant murmurs into her phone. She's unremarkable, thank god. And I have a new head shot pinned to my monitor.

Even if I hadn't told Sasha all those things, freely handing over pieces of myself like a love-struck idiot, the things I did are enough to ruin me.

Kissing her.

Touching her in the back of my car.

Spreading her open on that desk.

*Fuck.*

Those things didn't feel sleazy at the time. They felt—miraculous. Like being struck by lightning, over and over, my veins crackling with energy and light. But I can picture the headlines, imagine what she'll write, and I'm disgusted. With myself, with her… with it all.

"Well played, Sasha Jones."

I can't help but admire her cunning, if nothing else.

No one else ever got past my walls.

* * *

I break after two weeks. Two weeks of checking the headlines each morning, one eye screwed shut, a headache already squeezing my skull. Two weeks of *nothing*, barely a Google alert for my name, and I can't take it anymore.

Whatever she's got planned… it must be big.

It's bright when I step out onto the sidewalk. A clear day, the first in weeks, and watery sunshine bathes the street. I'd planned on taking the car, but when the fresh breeze ruffles my hair, I shove my hands in my pockets and set off on foot.

Spring is coming.

When did that happen?

A few people recognize me as I pass by, and I remember too late why I usually take the car. They blink, nudging each other and whispering, a couple even digging for their phones; they snap photos like I'm some wild animal, a panther escaped from the city zoo.

It's irritating. So stupid, I can't help but glare, but it's nothing out of the ordinary. They're not life-ruining-headlines stares.

Sasha's apartment is a half hour walk from the office. She walked this route so many times, in those merciless heels at first, and then in the sneakers I bought her.

It's pathetic, but I can't help picture it: her golden hair braided over one shoulder, or tied up in an intricate bun, glinting in the glass store windows as she strode along the paving stones. The scrape of her heels; that ridiculous bag weighing down one shoulder.

I imagine her hopping over puddles, weaving around street-lamps and bus stops, and without meaning to, I walk faster.

I'm going to speak to her.

That's all.

It occurs to me too late that it's past 9am on a Tuesday. She's probably at her job, her real job, typing up an article to ruin me, or else digging into some other poor bastard's business. But I'm almost there now, rounding the corner onto her street, and the only thing more ridiculous now would be to turn back without buzzing her door.

The steps leading to her building are pale stone. Washed clean by the rain. Black railings line the steps, wrapped in ivy vines. It suits her so well—classic but pretty—and there's an ache deep inside me when I ring her bell.

She won't be home, but I hover anyway, fists squeezing tight in my pockets. And as I rock on my heels, preparing to leave, there's a *click* and her voice floats through the speaker.

"Hello?"

"Sasha." Her sharp inhale makes me wince. Is she scared of me now? Was she always? "I'd like a word, if I may."

"S-sure." She unlocks the door with a buzz, but I shake my head, even though she can't see me.

"Maybe you could come down."

If I go up there, I'll never leave.

It takes an eternity for her footsteps to drift through the front door. How many flights does she live up? Does she not have an elevator? I back up to the edge of the stoop, forcing my face carefully blank, and wait for my first glimpse of her in weeks.

The door swings open.

My stomach swoops.

Sasha looks... wrecked.

Dark shadows cling beneath her eyes, while her normally pristine hair is scraped back in a messy ponytail. She's swapped her delicate blouses and pencil skirts for a paint splattered purple sweater and black leggings that wrinkle at the knee.

"Wow," I say flatly. "Betrayal suits you."

She doesn't even frown. That's how exhausted she is.

"What do you want, Grant?"

Sasha crosses her arms over her chest, leaning against the door frame like she can't keep up the energy up to stand. She watches me with those big brown eyes, so resigned, and I hate it.

But I can't fix this. Neither of us can.

"I want a warning. Call it a professional courtesy."

Her forehead creases. "I don't follow."

"Your article." I wave a hand between us, agitated. "Or exposé, or profile, or whatever it is you're working on. I'd like you to warn me before it comes out."

She raises an eyebrow. It's a flash of her old spirit. "So you can block it?"

"So I can brace myself."

She sags then, falling further against the door frame, all the stuffing knocked out of her. "Grant. There's no article. You can stop worrying."

"You expect me to believe that?"

She shrugs one thin shoulder. Has she lost weight? Is she eating?

"You can believe what you like."

And: no. That's bullshit. There's no way she's going to just sit on the things she dug up about me. My grudge over my parents' divorce—my brain injury—everything I did with *her,* all the while thinking she was my employee. It's all been whirling through my mind, keeping me up at night, chasing my steps on the treadmill.

Sasha Jones could wreck my business and make her own

career in one go.

Like hell is she not writing something.

"I can't believe *Simon*—" I can't help spitting his name, still jealous even now "—would let you waste two months undercover with nothing to show for it. He saw me holding your hand at the gala."

She frowns at the street past my shoulder. "I told him you were leading me through the crowd. That was all."

"And he bought that? It's a terrible lie."

She sighs. "Probably not. But he can't force me to write something against my will."

I stare at her, teeth grinding. Everything about her is so fucking sweet, even these lies.

"You look like shit."

A tired laugh bursts out of her. "Yeah. Thanks, Grant."

And I didn't mean it like *that*—she's still the most beautiful woman I've ever seen—but she looks worn down. Broken and hollowed out. So when I reach for her, hypnotized by the movement of my own hand, it's so easy to tuck her hair behind one ear. To brush her cool cheek with my knuckle.

Sasha's face crumples, and that's it. The tether inside me snaps, and I'm crowding her against the door frame, pressing our bodies together.

Her hands clutch at my shirt, dragging me closer, holding me near, and she buries her face in the hollow of my throat. Breathing me in. My jaw is clenched so tight my teeth ache, and her messy hair tickles my nose, and I've missed this so much. Her heat, her scent.

Sasha's breath puffs against my bare skin. She waits for me to do something. Say something. But I've got nothing. I'm coming up blank.

My instincts brought me here—closing the distance between our bodies. But now we're here, I've got nothing more to offer.

Sasha gives up first. She unwinds her arms from my waist, nudging me gently away. And when she peers up at me, her eyes are damp.

"There's no article. Stop worrying."

The door slams behind her, her footsteps creaking back up the stairs inside, and I stand rigid, the spring breeze kissing my cheeks.

No article.

Nothing to worry about.

I guess we'll see.

# Sasha

I lied to Grant. Again. But this time, at least, it was harmless.

There is an article. But it's not one the world will ever read. Simon kept pushing and pushing, stopping off at my cubicle or calling me into his office, and though I caved and wrote a series of pieces about the city's business scene to make Simon happy, I wrote something else too.

A piece about Grant.

Not for Simon's eyes. Not for *anyone's* eyes.

But in the end, I needed to write it down. For me. To make sense of the way my chest aches when I think of him; to acknowledge that I lost something real.

I stayed late one night at the Courier offices, tapping away at my keyboard with misty eyes. And then, when the night staff came in, I retreated back to my lonely apartment, with the string lights and shabby chic throws that Grant called me out for.

I wrote until the early hours of the morning, picking away

at it and honing like I was gunning for a writing prize. Not just trying to make myself feel better. And when I typed the last few words... something loosened in my chest.

Retreating back into my apartment after seeing Grant, my nerves all jangled up from his visit, my eyes snag on the laptop half-closed on my coffee table. I'm working from home today, part way through an article about corruption in the private school system, but my piece about Grant is still open on there too.

I pause beside the sofa. Chew my bottom lip as I lever the laptop fully open.

And with a muttered curse and a few clicks, I send it to him.

*Grant Keller: the Man Behind the Empire.* My love letter to the billionaire whose heart I broke.

I don't know why. It's not like he will ever read it. He'll probably take one look at the title and feel vindicated, so sure that I'm out to destroy his life. He's probably pinned my photo to that dart board in his office.

The front of my body is still flushed, overheated and hopeful from the way he crowded me against the door frame. And when I tuck my hair behind my ear, my fingertips brush a patch of skin *he* touched.

Oh hell. I'm spiraling. Mooning around my apartment over a man who hates me; hoping and yearning for a call that will never come.

That's not me. It's never been me, and I won't start now.

Sasha Jones is a fighter. An idiot sometimes, but a fighter nonetheless.

I stomp across my apartment and throw the curtains wide open, pale sunlight washing over the room. My sofa is a tangle of blankets and abandoned cardigans; there's a stack of books on the side table that I started and then tossed aside with a sigh.

No more. With a few grunts, I shove the window up a few inches too, and a fresh spring breeze floods inside. It tickles the leaves of my houseplants, and clears my foggy head.

Enough of this pity party.

It's time to move on.

\* \* \*

The press pool is packed. It always is when the city's bombastic mayor makes an announcement—he's a loose cannon. He could say *anything*.

So I'm crammed shoulder to shoulder with two other junior reporters, a notebook balanced on my knee and a recorder clutched in one hand. The crowd hums with noise, the podium at the front of the room standing empty, and I kick my leather bag under my chair as a man squeezes through our row.

City Hall. So many nights in college, I dreamed of this career. Getting out into the city, yelling questions on pale stone steps. The flash of bulbs and the scent of roasted coffee. My words in paper and ink, and flying digitally around the world.

It feels good. Working like this again—tuned in and excited about life. There's still a pinch in my stomach when I think about Grant, but I'm breathing better this morning. Sending that article to him helped..

"You think this is about the corruption scandal?" Francesca, a young reporter who started at The Courier the same month as me, leans close to mutter in my ear. Her dark hair brushes against my sleeve, and I shrug, tapping my pen on my notebook.

The mayor's office was cagey in their announcement. This could be about anything.

"Could be. Or could be nothing. A PR attempt."

She huffs a laugh. "What a waste of time. Simon would hate that."

I glance at her sideways—Francesca's cheeks are tinged pink. Another one bites the dust, falling for our stern, British boss. Maybe I'd have crushed on him too by now, if I hadn't met Grant. If my body and heart didn't sing out for another man.

"If there's no real announcement, that means this is a distraction. Which means there *is* a story, we just have to find it."

Francesca grins, nudging me with her elbow. "You're good at this."

My turn to blush.

The mayor enters ten minutes late—of course—striding to the podium like an Oscar winner collecting his award. He's in a burgundy three piece suit, an old-fashioned pocket watch chain dangling over his sizable chest, and it's easy to see how he climbed to power.

His voice rings through the room; his arms spread wide. This man is a showman to his bones.

I scribble notes on his appearance and demeanor and the possible subjects he came to address—or avoid. And I'm so wrapped up in what I'm doing that I don't notice the whispers rippling through the crowd. Not until a chair scrapes nearby, and Francesca mutters *holy crap,* and I raise my head to find Grant Keller at the front of the room.

He stands before the crowd, ignoring the outstretched recorders and yelled questions. The mayor gapes behind him, shocked into quiet for once, and Grant scowls as he scans the rows of fidgeting reporters.

Pale gray eyes land on me. My nerves crackle to life under my skin.

"Sasha?" Francesca whispers. "Is Grant Keller staring at you?"

I give a jerky shrug. I don't know. What the hell is he doing here?

But those eyes stay on me, burning and intense, and a muscle tics in Grant's jaw. He jerks his head to the doorway, urging me to follow, and then bodies are turning in their chairs, recorders thrust at me instead.

"Um."

I sit there like an idiot for a moment, the air in front of me bristling with recorders. But who am I kidding? I can't stay here now. Whatever nonsense the mayor wants to spin, I'll have to hope Francesca catches it.

My hands are clumsy as I scoop up my bag, shoving my notebook and recorder away. And for once, when I squeeze along the row, the other reporters move their freaking legs and let me by. A few even stand up to follow, and when I trail Grant out of the press room into a City Hall corridor, I'm not alone. Four male reporters follow me outside too, their recorders held aloft and a hungry light in their eyes.

Grant turns to face us. He crosses his arms, muscles bulging beneath his dove gray suit, and stares at the tag-along reporters for a short eternity.

They turn and leave, muttering under their breath.

"They'll still be listening." I feel like I should warn him. "And watching. You're far more interesting than the mayor."

Grant pinches the bridge of his nose. "Fucking press."

"Uh, Grant? *You* came here."

Another jaw tic. This is not going well.

And though I know he has every right to be mad, I'm really done with my penance. I apologized; I told him how I felt. I scooped my bleeding heart out with that article and sent it to him—the most vulnerable thing I've ever done.

If Grant Keller can't forgive me, he needs to leave me alone. So I tell him that.

"You think I haven't tried?" His words come out in a burst, and with a grimace, he lowers his voice. "I didn't want to come to your apartment. I didn't want to read that email. I definitely didn't want to come here."

It's not a declaration. It's not an offer of peace. It's nothing, and now Grant isn't the only one with a headache. I wince, rubbing my temple, and ignore the flash of concern on his face.

"I suggest a new hobby."

"What?"

"To help you resist temptation. Or maybe not a new one—maybe a suit-clad sprint on your treadmill will do it."

"So you don't want to see me," he says, voice flat. And that's the dumbest thing I've ever heard, even dumber than the mayor's awful opening jokes. My breath gusts out of me, my grip squeezing the handle of my bag, and I pin Grant with a glare to match his own.

"Grant? I *always* want to see you. Not seeing you every day has been killing me. But do I want you coming to my work, dragging me out of the press pool to tell me how much you wish you weren't here? No. I do not. If you don't feel the same way about me, that's fine, but this grudge—it's got to end."

As I talk, his face clears. He even stands taller, back straightening like a weight is lifting off his shoulders.

"Sasha. I've done this all wrong. I let my shitty mood take over."

I roll my eyes. "No kidding."

"Can I start over?"

"That depends. Will you be a jerk again?"

"No."

"Fine." I stare up at the ornate ceiling. City Hall is all pale marble and red carpets; shiny bronze sconces and oil paintings. It's a lot like the gala. "Go ahead."

He takes a deep breath. Then says it: "I love you."

At first, I think I heard him wrong. I jerk my chin back down, head spinning. But Grant keeps talking, and I'm *not* going insane.

"I love you, and I should never have stayed away so long. I thought—I thought that none of it was real. That you played me to get headlines out of me. But then I read your article, and…"

I swallow hard, face numb. "And?"

Behind us, the mayor drones into the microphone. The press pool rustles in their chairs, the sound floating through the polished wood door. Shoes click over nearby marble floors, and my breaths sound too loud to my ears.

Grant looks at me, so serious. He really does look like Clark Kent. Square-jawed and noble, his dark hair raked up like he's been tugging at it.

"And I believe you. I forgive you. I *want* you, Sasha Jones. I'm sorry it took me this long to say it."

It's okay.

It's all okay, because Grant is prowling forward, never mind the pairs of eyes watching us. He crowds me against the ornate wall, his big hands gripping my hips, his thumbs rubbing back and forth over the fabric of my suit pants.

I loop my arms around his neck, urging him against me, needing his warmth, and when his clean, masculine scent fills my nose, I finally relax.

"I'm supposed to be working," I mumble as Grant's lips sear a trail up my neck. His shoulders are so broad, they block out the weak electric lights.

"You are working." The words are hot in my ear. "Come with me and I'll give you the interview of your career. Even Simon won't complain."

I scoff at his harsh tone, a grin stretching my cheeks.

"Simon's a good guy, you know."

His low growl makes my toes curl.

"Come with me, sweetheart. I'll prove to you I'm better."

And, okay—the mayor's announcement is a bust. By now, everyone back at the offices will know that Grant Keller dragged me out of the press pool. I already have plenty of explaining to do, and if I'm screwed anyway...

Might as well go all the way, right?

I tangle my hand with Grant's. Rock up onto my toes and nip his bottom lip, tugging it gently with my teeth.

"Let's get out of here, Mr Keller."

He smiles at me, eyes crinkling.

"I thought you'd never ask that again."

\* \* \*

He promises me silk sheets and rose petals. Champagne and a bubble bath. But I've waited far too long for Grant Keller already, and the second we pile into the back seat of his car, I'm on him, crawling into his lap. The car pulls away, the driver's partition rising quickly to the ceiling, and I choke back a laugh at the scowl aimed over my shoulder.

"Sasha." He grips my hips, stilling me. "I told you, I'm going to do it right this time. Where would you like to go? We can go anywhere you like. The Four Seasons, Paris, Rome, my apartment—"

"Grant?"

"Yeah?"

"I want it right here."

He blinks, bemused, but there's hunger growing in his eyes, and his hands aren't still on my hips anymore. He's kneading me, rubbing my waist with his thumbs.

"… Right here," he repeats.

"Uh-huh." I roll my hips to demonstrate. And judging by the rock hard length beneath me, he's not as cool right now as he'd like to pretend. Just that hint of it, so big beneath my ass… I shiver, flashing hot under my clothes.

"We're in a moving car…"

"Never stopped us before."

"But it's your first time."

"*Grant*. It's with you. It's already perfect."

That softens him right up, the big idiot, emotion bleeding through his pale eyes, even as his movements get rougher. He rolls my hips *for* me, thrusting up to meet my core.

"Are you sure? Because once I get my hands on this pussy…"

I bite my lip, rocking harder. "Yep. Yes. Give it to me. I want it all."

Because that's what I want: Grant Keller out of control. The last threads of his restraint severed, and all that intensity aimed at me. And he doesn't disappoint—at my words, a shadow crosses his face, and he thrusts up rougher against me. Kneads my breast through my blouse, tweaking my aching nipple.

Then we're moving, the world shifting around us, and I'm tossed onto my back on the seat.

"The one time you don't wear a skirt," Grant growls, and then my pants are tugged open and yanked down my legs, tangling at my calves.

Grant buries his face between my thighs like a starving man. Mouthing at the lace of my panties; licking me through the fabric. And it's so much but not enough, and I'm writhing underneath him, begging but I'm not sure what for—

"This pussy is mine." He spanks it lightly, and I yelp. That quick sting spreads hot through my clit, my core, everything suddenly heightened. "*You* are mine."

"Likewise," I gasp, because I need to say something, need to stake my own claim, but my brain is frazzled. That little spank sent me offline.

"Obviously," he mutters, and then he's tugging my underwear down too, spreading me with his thumbs. Bearing down on me with his tongue, like he's determined to taste every last inch of me. Like he wants to swallow me whole.

And from the groans rumbling through his chest, from the way he settles further against the seat, he could happily just do this forever. Make me come over and over, wringing endless orgasms out of me until I melt into the leather seats—or die and go to heaven.

Well, that's no good. I want what I felt against his thigh—hot and hard and intimidatingly large. At least once before he kills me with his tongue, damn it.

"Grant." I pluck at his shirt, vision blurry as I stare at the car ceiling. "Fuck me. Please, I want you to fuck me."

He grunts and keeps licking. Slides a finger past my entrance, pumping slowly in and out. Outside, cars drift past on the street, and the shadows of pedestrians walk along the sidewalk, made fuzzy by the tinted glass.

*"Grant."*

He doesn't make me beg, thank god. He sits up, the movement sudden, his chin shining and his chest heaving under his shirt. I reach to pluck open a few buttons—god, I want my hands on that chest—but there's no time. He yanks my clothes off one ankle, undoes his belt with a clink, and then his cock is notched at my entrance.

"Fuck." He pauses, a shudder rolling through him. And his next words are bleak. "I don't have a condom."

"In there." I tug at the handle of my leather bag, dropped somewhere on the floor next to the seats. "After the first time we—well, I bought some. Just in case."

Grant pulls up my cavernous satchel, hope and despair mingling on his face.

"This ridiculous bag." He plunges in it up to one elbow. His muscles tremble where they meet my thighs—like he's vibrating from the effort of holding back. He's still notched against me, so freaking close.

"I know. It's too big."

"There's something fluffy in here."

"Hey! Eyes on the prize."

I know the exact moment he finds the condoms. He stills again, the humor draining from his face, and it's not funny anymore. Not when he tears open a packet, rolling one quickly down his length. Not when he presses against me once more and meets my eyes.

"Are you sure, sweetheart?"

So sure I might scream. My hips twitch, rolling a tiny

fraction, trying to urge him inside, and just the teasing brush of him—it makes my breath catch.

"Yes. So sure. Please, I want you—"

He eases in slowly. Inch by burning inch, the stretch emptying my lungs. I go stiff beneath him, and Grant pauses, dropping a kiss on my lips, rubbing soothing palms up and down my limbs.

"Relax. Let me in, Sasha."

"It's—you're *big*."

Grant huffs a short laugh. "I'm trying really hard not to be an ass about that declaration right now." He rolls his hips—not pushing deeper, just letting me feel him.

And *god*. Okay.

I see what the fuss is about now.

"Move." I tug at his shirt, too far gone for complete sentences. "Like that. Move."

He grunts and pushes forward another inch. The friction makes my body sing. The car rumbles beneath us, the engine purring as we coast along the road, and the sounds of the street outside are faint. Someone nearby leans on their horn.

It should ruin things. Should be unromantic, but when Grant pushes all the way inside, sealing us tight, it's so perfect my vision blurs. He's over me, around me, *inside* me, moving and gripping, and our breaths mingle in the tiny space between us.

He kisses me. Nips my lip like I did to him, then slides his tongue inside my mouth. And I've never been so owned, so taken over, so completely conquered, carried away by the sensations he's wringing out of my body.

"Sasha." He says my name like he's telling me a secret. Buries himself deep inside me—as deep as he can go.

He slides out. Pushes back in again.

Pumps in and out of me, over and over, washing over me and retreating like the tide. With every thrust, electricity crackles under my skin, his thumb dancing over my clit, and I never knew anything could feel this good.

The orgasm rushes over me. Slow at first, then unstoppable, urged along by his touch on my clit and his teeth on my neck. I still. I bite my lip. I *whine*.

And I clamp down hard on him, my legs shaking on either side of his hips.

Grant rides it out, staring at me like he wants to remember this more than anything. Every sensation and sound. And when I fall back, boneless, he thrusts once, twice more and swells inside me, coming with a shout.

It's messy. It's cramped. It's nothing like I'd imagined for my first time.

I wouldn't change a thing.

Grant cleans me up, then pulls my clothes into place. Deals with the condom then gathers me into his arms.

"So, that interview I promised…" He traces a line through my hair with his nose. I can feel his heart pounding under my palm.

I shrug. "We'll get to it. One day."

# Grant

*wo years later*

**T**Heads turn as I push through the Courier office doors, tired eyes blinking behind smudged glasses. They work hard here, I'll give them that. Every time I come to meet Sasha from work, half the reporters are draped over their desks, computer monitors flickering.

"Francesca." I nod at my wife's friend and colleague where she's leaning one hip against a desk. She grins at me as I stride past, her eyes twinkling.

"Good luck, Grant!"

I push on, ignoring the clench in my gut. I don't need luck.

These offices always startle me with how old-fashioned they are. Even with the latest tech humming from every desktop, the rooms feel stately. Old. With polished wood paneling on the walls, and checkerboard tiles, and shiny bronze light fittings. I half expect Sasha to step through a doorway, a gloved hand on her hip and an old-timey cigarette holder pursed between her lips.

Instead, I'm greeted by Simon.

The editor regards me closely, his cunning gaze raking over me from head to toe. No detail is missed; no weakness unnoticed. I ball my hands into fists in my pockets.

But I promised Sasha I'd do this, so I ignore the tension building in my spine and force a smile.

"Simon."

His mouth quirks. "Mr Keller."

He tips his chin, nodding toward the office behind him, and I follow through the doorway. The buzz of noise from the offices—ringing phones and tapping keyboards, grinding printers and low murmurs—it fades away as a heavy wood door swings shut behind me. Trapping me in here. With *him.*

And with the love of my life, a wry smile tugging her red lips. Sasha leans against the windowsill, her blazer rolled to the elbows and her legs crossed at the ankle. Her normal pencil skirt is gone, replaced with a stretchy fabric that hugs her rounded stomach.

"You're late, Mr Keller."

She winks, and the tension drains away. I blow out a long breath.

Sasha watches, hand drifting lazily over her blouse-covered bump, as Simon sits me at his desk. He places a recorder on the clean surface, empty except for a cup of pens and an old-fashioned paper planner, his monitor dark in the corner.

His chair creaks as he rolls closer. Uncaps a pen and digs in a drawer, before slapping a legal notepad down in front of him.

"Are you ready, Mr Keller?"

He asks the question, but it's her I look to. Sasha smiles at me, her soft expression hidden over her boss's shoulder, and gives a small nod.

"Yes." I clear my throat. "I'm ready."

It's the first real interview I've ever given. The first personal one, anyway—the first one that will leave me vulnerable. But Sasha insists that the world is changing, and the truth of my injury will be an inspiration, not the end of my career.

It might even help others in similar situations—might start a much needed conversation in the city and beyond.

When I first agreed, I wanted her to do the interview. But she smirked at me, leaned in close, and said: "I'm not really objective, Grant."

So Simon will do it, but Sasha will be here. And as my eyes flick to her now, I know that this will be okay.

*Trust me,* she mouths.

I nod at her.

I do.

\* \* \*

Thanks for reading the Grumpy Suits collection! I hope you liked it. :)

For another stern boss and his vengeful intern, check out His Last Nerve. *What does it take to break a man? I'm about to find out...*

And for more of Grant and Sasha, check out their bonus scene. *They've got unfinished business in that elevator...*

Happy reading!

xxx

# Teaser: His Last Nerve

When Levi Laurent moves through the building, we sense him coming from floors away. Papers rustle in people's hands, quivering with anticipation; drawers slam and desk chairs squeak.

The air changes, somehow, like everyone's holding their breath, just waiting for a glimpse of the boss. Hair is patted down, lipstick blotted, and ties are yanked straight. And when the elevator dings and *he* walks out, moody eyes scanning from left to right, the whole room fizzes with excitement.

Today is a prime example. I press myself back against the break room door, watching the boss get mobbed on his walk across the office, the clump of his admirers jostling the cubicle walls. He doesn't come to this floor too often—a detail which, had I known, might have changed my internship application.

I want to be near Mr Laurent as much as possible. But not for the same reason as these weirdos—no. It's so much easier to ruin someone's life from up close.

My palms are clammy, and I spread my fingers over the break room door behind me, leaning against the cool surface. Now that the boss is here, walking among us mere mortals, I can't tear my eyes away. Can't blink. Hot rage churns in my belly and tightens my chest, and my breaths come quicker.

Just the sight of him makes me want to scream like a banshee.

This asshole. This malevolent jerk.

Someone hands him a clipboard and Mr Laurent stops, frowning at the top page. His sensual mouth twists, and his frown deepens. Those sculpted shoulders are tense under his crisp white shirt, and he's several inches taller than the crowd.

I hate that he's so freaking attractive. I *hate* it.

He doesn't deserve that thick, wavy hair, sometimes brown or dark blonde, depending on the light. If there were justice in the world, this man would have only the thinnest strands of hair left—and he wouldn't be allowed to go bald with dignity. He'd have to comb those strands over every morning, staring into his own dead eyes in the bathroom mirror, wondering who he was trying to kid.

Is there a way to make a person go bald deliberately? Huh. I chew on my thumb knuckle, teeth digging in hard, and watch as he peels another page off the clipboard. It's a soothing thought.

Amid the cubicles, someone presses closer to the boss, like some of his talent might rub off on them. Gross. I roll my eyes and scoff under my breath.

You know, the people here worship Levi Laurent. It's completely genuine. They'd kiss the ground he walks on—hell, a few of them would probably lay flat and smooch it with tongue.

Why? As if I know. As far as I'm concerned, Levi Laurent crawled out of the smokiest depths of hell.

But it was startling on the first day of my internship, when I turned up in the smartest blouse I could find at the thrift store, all ready to rock and roll. I wanted vengeance, gossip, and one of those donuts in the break room for lunch. In that order.

I got my donut, at least. Vanilla icing with pink sprinkles.

But as for the rest? These people are disgustingly loyal, all staring after their evil boss like he hung the moon. Sure, he barks at them sometimes and they scuttle out of his way, but he's a *genius,* as they sigh to me during our lunchtime gab sessions.

Don't I know that Levi Laurent will save the world with his clean energy tech? Who wouldn't forgive a little grouchiness for that? And isn't he so *dreamy* with that faint French accent?

Vom. I want to learn his deepest fears, not that Angelica from legal is desperate to drop to her knees. She winked at me when she whispered that at Friday night drinks last week, like I must dream of crawling under his desk too.

Listen: the only thing I want to give that man is an ulcer.

I want him miserable, and I want to look into his tortured eyes so he knows it was me. That *I* did this… whatever 'this' turns out to be. The details of my vengeance are still hazy.

"These figures are wrong." Mr Laurent's deep voice cuts through the hum of conversation, and a few admirers step back, suddenly pale. The people in their cubicles turn back to their computer screens, and the sound of hurried typing rattles through the room.

Yeah, this is what happens when you worship a cruel, exacting god. You get your math wrong, and then bam! He smites you.

"We used the numbers your assistant Danny provided," a young man in a gray shirt says. He gives a sickly smile, but he's sweating. There are dark half-moons under his arms.

Levi's mouth purses as he frowns at the clipboard again.

God, a man with a full mouth like that shouldn't go around pouting. No wonder these idiots all want to nibble his bottom lip.

"Daniel gave you these figures?" he asks quietly. His voice is lowered, but it still carries.

Fevered nods all around. Poor Danny.

The boss mutters something under his breath, but I'm staring at his lips, so I mostly make it out. Something about *the third time this week.*

Yeesh. The clock is ticking on Danny.

A bolt of sympathy goes through me—I'm not a monster, okay?—but then I straighten against the break room door, my heart lurching faster. My teeth dig into my thumb knuckle, hard enough to sting.

Levi Laurent's assistant is about to get fired. There will be an opening on the top floor, up there with *him.*

Wrenching my hand away from my mouth, I tug my skirt straight. A plan forms in the back of my mind.

The clipboard is shoved back, the boss's path resumed. He cuts between a row of cubicles, calling: "Do it again. And check the figures this time." His crowd of admirers scatter like geese, feathers ruffled and eyes wide, but they won't blame him for any harsh words. Because he's such a dreamy genius, remember?

Bleurgh.

Why is he here? There's not much on this floor except admin staff, a row of copiers, and a water cooler. A few potted plants sag against the walls, their leaves pale with lack of sunshine. Sometimes I take pity on them, dragging them to the nearest window, but some asshole keeps moving them back.

Mr Laurent's path brings him past the break room. I paste a

polite smile on my face as he gets closer, trying to wipe away my rage and loathing. But I'm not sure I do a great job, because as he passes, the boss glances up—and our eyes meet.

He frowns.

And… *heat.* Searing heat crawls up my throat and cheeks. My heart pounds harder. My belly flutters, and my hands are slick as the room fades away. There's no shrill beep of copiers; no rattle of keyboards. Only the rasp of my breath. I'm woozy.

This is what hate feels like.

He's still staring as he draws level. I'm trapped, pinned by his gaze like a butterfly to a cork board. Or no, screw that, like something more dangerous…

Pinned like a scorpion with a dagger. Yeah.

Mr Laurent finally looks away, and I sag against the wood, light-headed. His broad shoulders slip through the doorway to a lawyer's office, and the whole room can breathe again.

God, I hate this guy.

"You get the figures!" A pair of accountants bicker in the middle of the room, shoving the clipboard back and forth like they're not grown-ass men. "Or better yet, wait until Mr Laurent hires an assistant with half a brain—"

I've heard enough. My back is damp under my blouse as I peel myself off the door. Time to write a flawless letter about how much I *love* Ignis Innovations and how I'd simply *die* for a permanent role. How it's my life's purpose to fetch a grumpy man coffee. Etc, etc, barf, barf.

Sorry, Danny. But I promise: I'll make him suffer for both of us.

\* \* \*

Check out His Last Nerve!

xxx

## Cassie Mint

# About the Author

Cassie writes outrageous, OTT instalove with tons of sugar and spice. She loves cookie dough, summer barbecues, and her gorgeous cat Missy.

**You can connect with me on:**

- https://www.authorcassiemint.com
- https://www.facebook.com/cassiemintauthor
- https://www.bookbub.com/authors/cassie-mint

**Subscribe to my newsletter:**

- https://www.authorcassiemint.com/newsletter